SECRETS OF A
DIRTY COP

SECRETS OF A

DIRTY COP

By Devon Sturdivant

Published by
MIDNIGHT EXPRESS BOOKS

SECRETS OF A DIRTY COP

ISBN-10: 0985768681
ISBN-13: 978-0-9857686-8-3

Cover art by Joshua Dunbar

Published by
MIDNIGHT EXPRESS BOOKS
POBox 69
Berryville AR 72616
(870) 210-3772
MEBooks1@yahoo.com

SECRETS OF A

DIRTY COP

By Devon Sturdivant

I would like to dedicate this book to the guys who once upon a time had dealing the law and still might be serving time because of an officer's abusive authority to get ahead in his career by using people for a stepping stone.

So, keep your head up and stay strong because it's a better time to come.

Acknowledgements

My mother Joan Sturdivant, James Sturdivant, sister Katy Denise Simmon Sturdivant, Brother David, brother-in-law Tyrone Simmon, Nephews Zackary Sturdivant, Mason Sturdivant, Trell Sturdivant, Antwan Anthony Sturdivant. To my kids Omar Sturdivant, Zavion Sturdivant, to my princess; Jade Sturdivant, along with her big sister Samaria Moore. My Cousin Trisha Sturdivant.

To my few good friends; Shane "The Boss" Hunt, Johnny Oxendine, Eric "Mack - Bone" Garner, Noland "Man"Justice, Ricky Walker, "DW Pageland, S.C" Carl Burgin, Mr. Rafael Diaz, Diane Sharpe, Gary Terrell, Russell Miller, Sacha Bond, Timothy Bond, Shun "The Great One" Audrey, Curtis Lyle, "Bear Tennesse Chattanooga," Ervin Royre, Jeffery Hamilton, Nate Bailey, Michael Author, Anthoney Peterkin, Divine Knowledge, Cavedric McNair, Randy Baker, Rachel Calhoun, Nelly "D-Town".

In memory of my little cousin, just want you to know that we love and miss you. God bless you. "Shelton Garon Sturdivant"

CHAPTER 1

(DISPATCH)

"We have a 911 emergency call," from a residential area of North Charlotte, Urban Community that is located in the Hidden Valley area on Pondella Drive. There has been a disturbance, possibly an assault on a female."

"Copied."

Dirty had earned that name from controlling the streets in the Black Community for almost 6 years by doing what fuck he wanted to do, from selling drugs to soliciting prostitutes, who pay for their freedom to walk the streets legitimately.

Carlos Bowman was his real name. He stood at 6'3" African American, who weighed approximately 228 pounds, built solid like a rock, with a low military hair cut.

Carlos had always been bothered since he was a kid and was old enough to understand the significant reason why many people loved crack cocaine. As a kid, he watched his mother smoke to her death. His father was in and out of prison. Carlo's considered him no earthly good.

Both parents combined were notorious in their own ways. But with his brain, he could conquer in 6 months what his parents couldn't do in a lifetime. Meet "Carlos," AKA Dirty. "I'm the fucking law."

"Hey you! Freeze" Dirty said, grabbing his walkie talkie. "Suspect is running on foot; need back up."

Dirty ran trailing the suspect only 10 yards behind him. He caught a break as the suspect tripped and fell over a log on the ground, in the wooded area they were running through. "You got me sweating like hell! Why the fuck you run? You bitch ass nigga!" Dirty said breathing heavy.

"I got your bitch, you pussy ass Cop!" the suspect said as he lay on the ground breathing hard.

"So you like hitting women! Shit!!!" You more of a bitch doing shit like that you faggot ass nigga," Dirty replied with a look and feeling inside that he could remember when his mother laid in the middle of the floor taking in her last breath.

As the suspect now was standing on his feet looking Carlos in his eyes, Carlos pulled his gun from his holster, when the suspect said "Ha, ha, like the bitch you are, you better had pulled out your gun!"

"I don't need my gun!"

"Put it down then!"

"Rip my badge off my shirt since that's what stopping your punk ass, fuck the gun! I don't need it."

The suspect reached and grabbed the badge and it fit perfectly inside of his palm. The suspect heavily sweated from his forehead, and squeezed the badge and pulled as the badge came off, ripping a hole in Dirty's shirt. There wasn't anything else to be said, but then the suspect spoke.

"Now what, Bitch?"

Pow, pow, pow! "Don't you know by now, niggaz don't fight fair no more you dead bitch!"

Carlos fell to the ground grabbing his own shirt and pulling it out of place. By this time the other Cops who arrived on the scene secured their own, regardless if they were wrong or right. It's a lot of shit the crooked Cops and good Cops have to go through in order to protect and serve. And what better way to do it and then to hide behind their badge that's set up like the shield that it is, and let Justice take its course.

TWO MONTHS RELIEVED WITH PAY

Carlos was rewarded with a paid vacation for killing another brother. And Justice had been served.

After returning back to work from the two long months of just laying around, Dirty thought how the first murder felt territorial, to ensure the neighborhood he didn't play games.

Dirty sat in the parking lot of the Countryside Apartment complex waiting on his drug dealer "Pat-Rat," to leave from his girlfriend's apartment, patiently waiting because the government wasn't giving up shit besides full benefits. And everybody that they kill is where the bonus comes from. That's why you should never pull over on a lonely road alone.

Finally, Dirty watched Pat-Rat lock the door of the apartment and jump in his $135,000.00 car pulling out and heading down N. Tryon going toward the Universe Area. Carlos turned his light on, trailed the car's bumper, and started blowing that loud-ass horn demanding Pat-Rat to pull over.

Pat-Rat pulled over as any Good Samaritan would do, not knowing why he was being pulled over. Dirty waited to get out of his cruiser, using one of the techniques all officers use before making a driver panic. "Making them Sweat" in order for them to get their lives together.

Dirty got out and looked himself over, brushing off the ashes from the blunt he had just smoked. He approached the window turning slightly to the side away from the window so he was able to pull his weapon at any given time.

"Yes Sir! What's the problem, Officer," Pat-Rat said politely.

"Let me see your driver's license and registration, please." Carlos asked.

"What happened, officer?"

"You ran the stop light! Are you in a hurry to be someplace?"

"Hah! It was green; I could've sworn it was green!" Pat-Rat replied like he was certain and not confused about the question.

Dirty went back to his police car then handing his registration and license back, Dirty said. "I see you've had a previous drug conviction?"

"Yeah, but what does that have to do with me running the red light as you proclaimed?"

"Get out and stand right there in front of your car please sir; put your hands on the hood." Dirty watched Pat-Rat until he stood there right where he wanted him.

CHAPTER 2 - BLUE LIGHT

Dirty now was inside the vehicle. He opened the arm rest was a large amount of cash. As he proceeded to check under the seat, Dirty found a gun. And when he came up for air, Dirty put the gun and two ounces of crack on the hood of Pat-Rat's car.

Immediately, Pat-Rat said, "That's not my crack. The gun is, but you had to put that shit there," he said with a facial expression that it might be over for him.

"Look, I thought you were smarter than the thugs that wear their pants hanging off their asses."

"Man, c'mon don't do me like that now," Pat-Rat cried.

"Put your hands behind your back."

"Can I call my lawyer?"

Dirty put Pat-Rat in the back seat of the police car and closed the door. Then Dirty grabbed his cell phone and called one of his friends that worked at the wrecker towing spot that was located on Sharon Amity to impound the vehicle, and make sure nobody touched anything.

Jumping in the police car, Dirty pulled off going down 49 toward Concord Mills when Pat-Rat's phone started ringing. "You expecting a call?" Dirty asked.

Nah, but why are we going in the opposite direction from the jail?"

"So we can talk!"

Dirty pulled in at Wal-Mart and parked. Dirty had a proposition for Pat-Rat; whether he accepted it or not, it was up to him. This was going to determine whether he ever walked the streets of Charlotte again.

"Do you wanna go to jail?" Dirty asked.

"No!"

"Look! I'm not going to put all my time into something I have control over, either you make me some money or you will go to jail! Do I make myself clear?"

"How am I supposed to do that, when my connect is supplying me?"

 "Your phone is ringing again, hold on."

Dirty got out and took the cuffs off Pat-Rat and handed him his phone. He dialed the number back. On the other end of the phone was Pat-Rat's man.

Finally, they came to an agreement. Dirty decided to give back the money he took from the glove-compartment. The large amount was just a small portion compared to what Pat-Rat had in the trunk of his car that Dirty didn't know about.

Dirty took Pat-Rat to the towing service, were they traded information, and Pat-Rat left to go meet his dealer.

(DISPATCH)

"We have a 911 emergency call on Eastway Dr. and the Plaza Rd, at the shopping Center. There is a robbery at the Bi-Low's grocery store. Suspect is still believed to be inside, Black male wearing a baseball cap, black shirt, blue jeans."

"Copied," Dirty replied almost five minutes away from the shopping center.

Dirty was the first to arrive at the scene. He spotted the suspect as he tried to blend in with the citizens. Dirty drove as if he wasn't paying the suspect any attention.

The suspect pulled off just as four other cars arrived. Dirty followed the car as he pulled off driving down Eastway Drive. Before the suspect could approach the red light, Dirty turned his lights on demanding that the suspect pull over.

Cautiously, Dirty walked to the vehicle with his gun inside his hands, and screamed.

"Put your hands on the steering wheel now!" By this time, Dirty had opened the car door, grabbed the suspect by the shirt and pulled him out of the vehicle, putting his arms behind his back and hand-cuffing him.

Finally, Dirty had the suspect in the back of his car and then called for backup. Before the other police had arrived, Dirty took half of the weekly earnings out the bag that Bi-Low's had put up in the safe waiting for the Brink's truck to pick up for deposit.

After taking the suspect downtown for booking, the other officers congratulated Dirty for his outstanding and successful arrest.

Dirty left the police station and went home to be with his wife and son. Once in his office in the basement of his house, Dirty counted the money he had stolen. He came up with a total of $50,000.00 which was a helluva come-up doing nothing but protecting and serving.

Dirty heard the bell ring from upstairs that someone wanted to get buzzed downstairs where he was at. Dirty quickly closed the safe, and made sure everything was in place, including the two ounces of crack that he framed on his prime suspect.

Whoever it was wanted into the basement, and he sat as if he was studying. Sophelia, his beautiful wife of twelve years, came in. She had a body to make the average stripper kneel down at her presence.

"Hey Honey, how was your first day back at work?" Sophelia still asked and was concerned about the shooting that had occurred in the past leaving a young man dead.

"It's hard! Especially dealing with cats' you don't know what's the next move. I'm just staying focused so I'm able to watch my back and others that may be in harm's way," Dirty said, confusing his wife with his character as well as his demeanor. Sophelia really did not know the man she had married.

CHAPTER 3 - TWO DAYS LATER

Dirty hadn't heard a word from Pat-Rat. He didn't know if Pat-Rat thought he could drag him along or what. But Dirty sat there in the living room waiting patiently for Pat-Rat to arrive at his girlfriend's apartment.

"I called his number and he's not picking up," Justine said.

Because Dirty ensured her that he was on his way, she knew it wasn't likely for anyone to show up and to meet Pat-Rat at her place. But he introduced himself as Carlos.

Justine was 5'3" yellow red bone, who worked at the bank uptown. She was so thick, her ass moved bouncing with every step she took. Justine had a long pony tail and looked as if she were very conservative.

"Look, I could leave and come back if it's inconvenient for you? I will try his number once more, damn it's still busy."

"No, you don't have to leave, he should be here any minute," she said as if she was becoming enticed by Dirty's charm.

Dirty had won her attention with his $90 thousand dollar truck he parked in front of her door. For two weeks Pat-Rat had ducked and dodged him.

After about two hours, Dirty had Justine laughing and going on. They now sat at the kitchen table drinking Hennessey while listening to Avant.

They both were sitting there laughing as Justine revealed her beauty. She had some perfect white teeth.

Dirty asked her did she smoke weed, and to his luck she did. He pulled out a sack and a blunt started rolling.

"That looked like it might be some hydro," she said being curious.

"I admit you most definitely know your weed. Can I ask you a question?" Dirty looked with this interested, charming smile as he gazed in her eyes.

"Yeah. What is it?" She was now feeling comfortable with Dirty.

"Just how you know your weed! What about your man?"

"What that's supposed to mean?"

Dirty took a deep pull and inhaled, knowing he had to answer something to what he just said. Then Dirty handed the blunt to her as he still held his smoke, holding up his finger, saying hold on for a second. Justine took a pull and smoked like she had been doing it for a while, when Dirty said "Some women don't know their man, especially when they are trying to be at two places at one time. I used to be that person who wanted his pie and eat it too."

Dirty must have touched a nerve, because Justine just sat back in her chair, so relaxed that she burned the blunt almost completely up.

Then Dirty heard some keys. When he turned, Pat-Rat came through the door, spotting Dirty sitting at the table with his woman.

He tried to control himself but was shocked and surprised. Quickly, Dirty jumped up, and showed Pat-Rat some love and whispered to him, "How can you be so damn stupid? Act like you know or else," Dirty said out loud.

"Nigga! I've been here almost three hours, when you told me this three hours ago, that you were on your way!"

"Yeah. Umm. …C'mon let's do this. Let me grab something and I'll be ready. What's up, Baby?" Pat-Rat said disturbed and all discombobulated.

When Pat tried to kiss Justine, she pulled away. Pat was so mad that he let her win without defending himself, making her curiosity run wild with what Dirty had said about being in two places at one time.

Pat went upstairs, while Dirty went over to shake her hand. She extended it and Dirty held hers in his hand meaningfully as he was trying to spark a fire that needed to be put out. Justine watched Dirty with her unbelievable eyes that told him more about why she wished that it was him instead of Pat right now. Finally they heard footsteps and released each other's hands.

Dirty had a way with breaking up a happy home.

Once they got outside you could see the steam coming from Pat's head.

"How the fuck you know where my girl live?" Pat said.

"Cause I am the muthafucking law, that's how you shit head muthafucker! Now let's get something clear. You don't hang your phone up for two weeks and think what happened between us was a dream. This here is real, and you better wake your ass up, and get on the ball, because my patience is limited. If this happens again, kiss your black ass goodbye. Shit. …You make an officer think you trying to set him up! Remember, you can't be at two places at one time."

Dirty left leaving Pat-Rat standing looking like what the fuck he'd gotten himself into. Dirty went on Sugar Creek Rd, and spotted a couple of bad-ass bitches looking as if they were prostitutes. Dirty thought how he'd never seen them around here before. Good thing his wife was out of town.

Dirty pulled over at the service station. He looked nothing like a cop off Duty. Dirty won people with his charm and ability to be outspoken in character.

Dirty came out of the station from paying for his gas. Outside the door the ladies were standing there when he came out. "What's up ladies?" Dirty said, being in one of his flamboyant moods.

The girls didn't waste any time. "Shit! What's the business?" the girls said being up front and direct with what they wanted.

Dirty wasn't about tricking, every dollar he needed including the gasoline that went inside of his gas tank. "Where the fuck you hoe's from?" Dirty said pumping these hoe's adrenaline to get money.

"We from New York, that why you haven't seen real hoe's around here nigga! We locking this shit down around here," they said laughing together.

"Y'all riding with me?"

"You want both of us?"

"Bitches, I live life to the fullest. Now, bring y'all stink ass on!"

Dirty realized he never asked the hoe's their names because it really wasn't important; he had his significant other at home.

Both hoes were "Red", which is a turn on for any average nigga. Monica was 45 around the ass with a head full of weave, a pretty girl with a lot of war paint (make-up). She stood at 5'10" and most definitely was about a dick.

Then you had the shot caller, the head bitch in charge. "CeCe," who was short like 5'1" mostly with a natural appearance; a typical black woman who knew about her morals and selling pussy was strictly business.

CHAPTER 4 - HOES

Dirty was in denial about getting a room purchased. He convinced these hoes it was more money in it for them using their own spot. Monica and especially CeCe who were skeptical about the whole situation, but Dirty confided into these tricks so much they trusted him. Every word he chose to say patch a spot within them that Dirty healed.

Once inside the room, Dirty noticed the suitcase on top of the double bed.

"Dirty!" Where did you get that name from?" CeCe asked.

"Why your little ass got to know everything? You need to get naked so I can fuck the shit out of your ass."

"Nigga, please! You talk like you got a King Kong dick." Monica replied anxious to see it.

"Hold the fuck up! Where's the money? You know we charge $200 dollars each," Monica said demanding hers before anything happened. "Dirty, can I hit that blunt?" Monica asked.

"Yeah, but I'm taxing your ass later for it."

Monica thought what that was supposed to mean.

Dirty pulled off his clothes and hung below was 10 inches of beef. He laid back on the bed putting his rubber on while the girls eyes were fascinated with what they were seeing.

"Damn! Dirty. You holding plenty meat between your thighs," said Monica now sitting on the side of the bed jacking his dick up and down and analyzing what she was about to get.

Dirty looked real close at their naked bodies trying to spot anything that looked abnormal. CeCe looked if she was trying to stay away from the activity that was going on, but Dirty had something in store for her little short ass. "Money." He was going to get his money's worth.

Monica straddled Dirty's dick. She was so wet that his dick sunk partially half way before hitting a muscle. She had to work her big thick ass-cheeks to loosen her pussy enough so that Dirty's dick worked itself inside her tight pussy. "Hmmmm...Baby. Damn, you hurting me poppa. Oh shit," Monica said while riding his dick, rotating her hips like she was a professional. The pussy got good and wet.

CeCe had dropped in between his legs and under Monica's ass-cheeks licking Dirty's balls as she put them in her mouth as Monica hogged the dick all to herself. "Damn Pop-pa. I'm cumming..." Monica said.

Dirty couldn't hold back, gripping her hips as they both came.

Dirty changed rubbers, grabbed CeCe's hand and said. "Bring your little ass here and let me get my money's worth, you little trick," Hoes liked the talk.

Monica went to the bathroom to take a shower.

"I'll be what the fuck you want me to be as long as you paying, nigga!"

"You a little shit talkin' bitch! Lay on your stomach."

"Damn! Hold up, I am," CeCe looked to make sure Dirty had his rubber on.

Dirty laid across her on her back and wrestled for a minute with her, until he entered CeCe's little pussy.

"Oh, God! Damn it. You hurting me," CeCe cried.

Dirty gripped the top of her head so he was able to brace himself while he tried to touch inside CeCe's stomach.

"Ow! You hurting me," she said as Dirty kept pumping.

His rubber busted and she could feel the real thing inside of her. "Dammit! Stop! Stop!" she begged.

"Oh Yeah! Hold on then." Dirty's dick was good and wet. He grabbed his dick and forced it into CeCe's ass.

"Stop it," she cried as Dirty's heavy body pressed against her so that it was impossible for her to move.

He entered her ass and fucked her little butt cheeks and she cried tears like a river coming off a cliff. "What's wrong trick? Big girls don't cry." He said as he kept putting that dick inside her.

Just then Dirty felt a barrel against his head.

"Get the fuck up off her right now, son-of-bitch! Get your ass up!"

Dirty felt the steel budge hard on his skull and said. "Alright, alright. Hold up, I'm coming out!" Dirty replied as he got up with the rubber rolled back around his dick to his pubic hairs

"Get your shit on and get the fuck out of our hotel nigga! You got us fucked up bitch!" Monica said, very upset and concerned about her girl who was just stuck under this big-ass nigga.

"So, that's how you hoes like to play? What about my refund, tricks?" Dirty asked highly upset.

"Only refund you gonna get is some buckshot in your ass, nigga! Now, get the fuck out." CeCe said rubbing her little butt cheeks.

"You know, it's against the law to carry a gun," Dirty said on the way out of the door, laughing.

Dirty left heading home to wash his ass. Dirty thought how those hoes didn't give him all his money's worth, but he laughed because the surprise he had for them could send them off on a trip like if they took some acid.

Dirty's wife was out of town with her new job training and an opportunity for a better job.

The hot water in the shower ran as the steam filled the bathroom. Dirty called his son who was with his grandparents.

Little Carlos, Jr., who was only six years old, and since his birth, he spent most of his quality time with his grandparents.

The water splashed Dirty's body as he relaxed himself and thought how it was possible that he may have problems with Pat-Rat, but it wasn't anything he couldn't handle. Dirty knew it was Pat's life sentence and not his own.

One of Dirty's informers gave him the information that he had on Pat-Rat and the address of his girl where he spent most of his time.

Turning the shower off as he dried off he just wanted to lay down because tomorrow he would have a 12-hour shift and a few places he had to go and check out.

16

CHAPTER 5 - EMERGENCY CALL

(DISPATCH)

"All Units, we have several black males in the Hidden Valley area shooting at a police car along Tom Hunter and Vancouver.

"Copy! On the way"

Once Dirty arrived there were 20 other cars in position where they blocked the entrance coming and going. Dirty thought this was the fun part about catching any nigga with two legs and two arms; they were able to beat a nigga until he had one of each. If he'd lost his life, then oh well.

Dirty thought he was far from being a "hero". He cared nothing about front row center. A dead man to him was lifeless, barren, and a dead soul. Ain't good for shit. White people claim they don't want nothing to do with black, but they got your liver and lungs smoking that away.

Dirty assumed his position with his gun drawn to anything that didn't have any business moving. If so, they were dead. The ambulance finally came and got the wounded cop who was shot in the arm. This community was infested with gangbangers, Crips and Bloods mixed all in one hood, and they were killing each other. The boom squad arrived, one of Dirty's favorite rescues; they just go in and get your ass, then the party is over with. At the end of the day, nobody else get killed.

A hundred police surrounded one house. There was no possible way out unless they had an underground tunnel, but Dirty knew they weren't that smart.

Just minutes later, the bomb squad kicked the door in where they were told four guys were seen running in the house. Dirty and other cops covered the premises, securing the ground for anybody who wanted to try getting away on foot.

They apprehended five kids, none of whom were 17, but who were already trained to kill anything or anybody who crossed their territory.

The Hidden Valley Kings "PeeWee," all had dreads hanging below their shoulders and pants that hung off their asses. Three of the young men that were apprehended already had bodies (murders) with tear drops on their faces to proclaim they had taken a life.

Dirty backed out of the driveway and thought he would pay a visit to the young women who owed him a refund for some ass he didn't get to finish.

After pulling in the parking lot of the hotel, Dirty knew it wasn't likely that they would've kept the same room. If they did, the bitches were hit.

Dirty slowly rode through the parking lot. He saw just few housekeepers and not many people.

It was lunchtime on Friday. Dirty knew there was money to be made. After passing room 425, it looked as if nothing was happening. He'd have plenty time to roll on them hoes, so he went back to the station.

Dirty had Justine on his mind. For some reason, he took a liking to her. From what he had gathered, she was a woman that throbbed off drug dealers. Get what you can, Dirty thought. It wouldn't be right if she didn't. "Justine Black" born and raised here in Charlotte North Carolina, (Queen City).

Dirty pushed her name through the computer. There she was a picture of herself. An old ticket for speeding, current address was Countryside

Apartments. Now Dirty thought 'how was he going to pressure Pat-Rat for the cake (money). Because his time was limited, and he didn't have time for games. So, he called Pat-Rat up.

"Yeah! What's up?" Pat-Rat asked as if he was fed up.

"I don't like your attitude! You act if this shit is a game, muthafucker! I'm the law, and I set principals around this bitch!"

"I don't care what kinda principals you set, you better stay the fuck out from around my bitch!" Pat replied like his last nerve had built up so much from being frustrated that he wanted to kill Dirty's ass.

"Em.... it's like you got a lot of hostility built up in you. Fuck, nigga! You think them crackers give a fuck about me putting a bullet in your ass or putting you behind bars for the rest of your life? Huh, nigro? I don't want your bitch! Get me my Money! I got a bitch, and it would take 5 Justine's to compare to my wife!" Dirty said with a lot of rage in his voice hoping it didn't have to come to this.

"I hope and pray that you didn't tell my girl that I'm working for the police?" he said all discombobulated, as if right now he could be suicidal.

"Meet me at T.G.I Friday's at 8:00 p.m. on W.T. Harris." Click!

Dirty thought there was more he needed to do to catch this nigga's undivided attention. He wasn't about to babysit no grown-ass man. He controlled his area as he thought how time was dragging slow.

Dirty was able to go home, shower, and shit. Before he decided to leave, Dirty went downstairs to the basement, and opened the safe to grab a bag of "Hydro." He was getting low on his product. Dirty had jacked some young kids for it; he confiscated their stuff instead of taking them to jail.

Dirty knew he had to be careful with this scared-ass dude. It was something about Pat-Rat that he felt wasn't right. Dirty was hood something he could never stop being, living in and out of foster homes, and getting abused.

Dirty sat in the parking lot and looked around to observe the area and looked for Pat-Rat's car but it was nowhere in sight. He decided to call him; it as 8:15 p.m.

"Yeah," Pat-Rat said.

"Where you at playboy?" Dirty asked trying to comfort him with a sense of humor.

" I'm here! Inside, waiting on you!"

"There's been a change of plans. Come across the street to Chili's. What are you driving?"

"A black Dodge Stratus."

Dirty hung up and went to the location. This time, he waited inside the restaurant. He looked for himself and checked out the scene. Then, Dirty received a phone call.

"Yo J.J. What's up, nigga?" Dirty asked, excited to hear from his old partner in crime.

"This cat you messing with. I'm assigned to this dude and he's trying to put you in the cross."

Dirty listened to his partner's information when Pat-Rat walked inside. The instructions that Dirty had gathered from J.J. were not to conduct any business as of yet. J.J. was supposed to confirm with the Captain the allegations that Pat-Rat stated were true, and this was a regular routine

20

for them both, not trusting their hoodlum, and extorting them for their drug money.

"Yo. What's up cuz!" Dirty asked playing it off.

"Ain't shit! Besides, you trying to set a nigga up?" Pat asked with this smug look on his face like he wasn't going to let a cop play him for what he had.

"What? We're family. Have you lost your mind? I'm sorry you feel that way. I'm out cuzo," Dirty said leaving Pat-Rat behind telling him to forget the cookout this weekend.

Then Pat-Rat screamed out, "Why the fuck you keep calling then? Huh?"

Dirty continued walking and didn't bother to look back at his disgusting-ass, very disappointed that Pat-Rat was a snitch and tried to double-cross him but Dirty knew that was nothing compared to the "Triple Cross".

Devon Sturdivant

CHAPTER 6 - NEXT DOOR AT WORK

Dirty controlled the "Hidden Valley Area" where all the gang members where having shoot-outs, stabbing and killing each other just for recreation.

Dirty parked in the cut of a dead-end street, and called J.J. to meet at their old spot. Dirty thought that it wasn't good for anybody to know his business, not even another crooked-ass cop. Dirty knew he wouldn't tell on himself.

Finally, J.J. arrived. He pulled up and got out of his forty-five thousand dollar truck. He got in with Dirty.

"What's up Dirty?" J.J. asked as they shook hands.

"What's happening? Give me the run down with the administration, are they in my business?"

"The captain is like us; once upon a time, he worked these streets like we're doing now. It's just that you need to cover your steps."

"Yeah, yeah. I heard a lot about the Captain, but this dude Pat-Rat, I've never experienced anyone like him before. Normally, niggas are happy to have a cop behind their back, throwing them some shit to get on. But apparently, this guy isn't trying to share his wealth," Dirty said. His stay was cut short when a call from the dispatch came over his radio.

(911 DISPATCH)

"We have a 911 emergency call from Food Lion on Plaza Rd. Two suspects stealing from the grocery store, one believed to be wearing a baseball cap with dreads and the other one is a female wearing black pants and a red top."

"Copy! I'm on my way."

Dirty figured he would just go pick them up and take them someplace for target practice. Once Dirty arrived, the manager came outside pointing in the direction in which they left walking. Dirty drove down the street and just as the dispatcher had described what the suspects had on, he quickly pulled in behind them and got out.

"Come here you two." Dirty pointed as they stopped.

"Yeah, officer. How can we help you?" the older man asked looking like he had been smoking crack.

"Y'all been stealing? Don't lie! Just give the people's shit back so I can return it."

"We ain't got nothing officer," the crack-heads pleaded.

"Turn around and put your hands on the hood. Now, if I find anything, you're going to jail! Do I make myself clear?" Dirty asked while giving search and patting the female down.

The crack-heads didn't have anything on them, so Dirty refused to take them back. He told them to get out of dodge then walked back up the street looking along the side of the road. Dirty came up to some bushes and saw a big brown paper bag laying there.

Inside the bag were some steaks, pork chops, hamburgers, beef and all the meat you could possibly name.

Dirty picked up the bag and walked with it. The couple looked as if they were sick that Dirty found the merchandise. He laughed and waved at them as he put the bag inside his trunk.

He then passed them saying, "I'm taking this home!"

"Wait! Hold on please," the female said.

Dirty stopped and waited until she caught up with the car, then started to pull off in one of his playful moves. Dirty rolled down the window.

"Can I suck your dick for a few dollars? Please, I'm sick," she said.

"Yeah! You've got to be sick asking a police officer of the law to get his dick sucked. But I tell you what, suck on my black jack until it nuts. Come here and reach your face in the car. Yeah, that's it. Open your mouth. C'mon, open it. Here suck on it. There you go, baby. Yeah. That feels good. Hmmm....make it a little bit wetter."

Dirty pushed his black jack in and out of her mouth. She wasn't that bad looking for a crack-head. You could tell she hadn't been on it for a while, she was strung out and couldn't control her addiction. Dirty pushed the black jack in further down her throat, almost making her throw-up.

The girl's lips were a natural pretty pink and not yet scarred. Her hair was stringy and out of place as if she belonged to someone.

The nigga she was with, who was having her trick to support his habit, stood out of the way and watched.

Finally, about ten minutes of sucking on the hard steel, she looked as if she felt ashamed of what she had just done.

She had the most perfect teeth Dirty had ever seen; she looked more like a housewife.

"What's your name?" Dirty asked.

"Regina!"

"Here, take my business card. When you get straight and you are able to talk, and not high, call me. Here's $20. There's more where that came from; you hear me?"

"Yeah!"

As Dirty drove off, he looked in the review mirror. Old boy was trying to take her money. Dirty thought they had problems of their own just like he had.

"911 (DISPATCH"

"There's been a disturbance on Timmbrook and East-way behind Garringer High School, a man is jaywalking."

"Copy! I'm on my way."

"Damn! Dirty thought how he didn't have any time for himself and a life of a whole lot of trials-and-tribulations that he'd allowed himself to be a part of as a counselor for the streets.

When Dirty arrived on the scene, there in front of him was a man that probably couldn't have been 32 years old and was ass naked.

"Hey. Hey. Bring your ass here!" Dirty said walking toward the naked man.

"Hey, hey, hey," the man repeated himself, repeating what Dirty had said.

"What's wrong, sir? Why are you walking up and down the street butt-ass naked? You can't do that shit!" Dirty realized he was wasting his breath, because dude was on a trip; he had gotten hold of some bad drugs.

People gathered around as Dirty placed him in the back seat of the car and called an ambulance. Dirty walked over to some of the civilians and tried to get a better understanding of what happened. The people pointed to a drug house forty yards down the street in the cul-de-sac.

When the ambulance arrived, Dirty transferred the naked man to the back of the meat wagon and then got back in his cruiser, drove to the cul-de-sac and peeped the house. He turned around in the circle and left the neighborhood.

Dirty headed to the hotel where the hoes strolled on Sugar Creek across the bridge going over hwy 85. When he got there, he sat in the parking lot facing the room he was in earlier; Dirty didn't know for sure if they still lived there.

It'd been a long day. Dirty was tired and exhausted. He thought by the time he was done with these hoes and Pat-Rat, they would deify him.

CHAPTER 7 - HOTEL

Right when Dirty was about to leave, a taxi pulled up, and to Dirty's surprise, CeCe and Monica got out.

Monica and CeCe looked totally different from the hoes on the strip. They watched the police car as they got their bags out of the taxi and but didn't realize it was Dirty.

Dirty put his cop hat on and got out. He followed the females, staying far enough behind them that they had time to slide the card and get inside. Before they could close the door, Dirty forced his way in through.

"Hey! What are you doing? You don't have a search warrant!" CeCe cried before realizing it was Dirty.

Removing his hat, Dirty said "I don't need no damn warrant! Back your little ass out of the way and turn and put your hands behind your back."

Dirty handcuffed both women and sat them on one of the beds alongside some luggage.

"Man. You mean to tell me you're a fucking whore cop?" CeCe said mad as hell with Dirty who was going through everything that they owned.

"Yeah! I am a fucking whore Cop! I had to test that ass before I decided to put it up for marketing."

"I run this area and no bitches tax me for ass, then put the steel up against my head. That's attempted assault on an officer with intention, not intent, but intention to kill!"

"I should've killed your ass, up in my girl, I was scared the bullet might have kept traveling and hit her, but then again, we wouldn't have had to worry about your Dirty ass! We've seen plenty cops like you from where we from." Monica said highly upset.,

"Dirty, not Dirty azz! Trick, it's time I stop being too soft on you muthafuckers.'"

Dirty figured he done lost more money than he had gained. He went through everything and sat all of it on the dresser. There was a .38 pistol, x-pills, marijuana and about $12g's in cash money.

Monica had tears dripping from her eyes and CeCe was shaking her head like she was hysterical.

"I told your ass it was against the law to carry a firearm. You can get 15 years for this tool (gun). C'mon; get y'all asses up."

"C'mon, please? We'll do anything. Don't take us to jail," CeCe begged along with Monica.

Dirty remembered that last muthafucker who tried him the same way, and he didn't get shit from it. He escorted them out the hotel room and put the ladies in the back seat of the police car, closing the door behind them.

He had all the evidence in the front seat in a plastic bag. Dirty wrote his report then called in and let the Dispatcher know he was bringing in two.

Dirty pulled off and thought how good it felt to be doing his job. Once down town before going in the intake Dirty said, "When you ladies make bond, that's *if* you make bond, you broke-ass bitches, call this number and your luggage will be there. If you lose it, then it's someone else's. So your property is safe. Here you go. Well, wait until I take the cuffs off.

"Fuck you Pig! You fucking dickhead," they both screamed realizing what had happened.

Dirty handed his gun in through the window were all weapons go. Then he walked them through the sliding door. After taking the cuffs off, he handed them the number, then the Sheriff took the girls while Dirty went to the magistrate with the forms. They stared at Dirty and gave him the middle finger while he winked his eye, then left. He didn't wanna be in there no more than they did.

* * *

DIRTY AT HOME

After Dirty got out of the shower he relaxed while drinking a cold beer and watching T.V. waiting on his family who should be coming home at any moment.

Dirty's main focus was Pat-Rat and how he was going to trick his ass. Dirty was mad enough to shoot that nigga with Pat-Rat's own gun that he had found under Pat's car seat. But he wouldn't because Dirty had other plans for this particular matter.

Just then Dirty heard a vehicle in the yard. He rushed to his feet and got himself together, then ran to the door and went outside to meet his beautiful wife and son.

His son screamed, "Hey, Daddy! Hey, daddy!" His son was so happy to see his father.

"Hey son, you miss me?" Dirty asked as he gave his son a high-5.

Sophelia had been training and her build was unbelievable, Dirty thought.

He picked up his son and took him in the house to tuck him in for bed.

Once Dirty had his son asleep, he rushed back downstairs to the basement while his wife took a shower. He opened his safe and fired up an already-rolled blunt.

There's something about what hydro does to him (marijuana). Once he finished, he turned the air on so the smoke was able to circulate out of the room into the vent.

Dirty quickly ran upstairs to their bedroom. He no longer heard the shower on so he pulled off his shorts and laid there on his back with his dick touching the sky.

The door opened and Sophelia walked through the door in her birthday suit. The muscles in her thighs ripped in every part of her body that showed. The hair between her legs was curly and neatly trimmed. Her beautiful nipples stuck out as far as a pencil eraser; nice sized breast; just two hands full.

Sophelia dove forward like a wild woman and cuffed her husband 10" inch dick and deep throated it, gagging with each stroke, moving her head side-to-side like she knew that she owned the dick. She caressed Dirty's balls in the other hand.

Dirty knew not to touch her head while she worked. She was now on both knees where she braced herself between Dirty's thighs, with his dick still down her throat, controlling every moment. The muscles in her shoulders and neck flexed; she didn't have an inch of fat nowhere.

Dirty extended his arms with his fingers spread out as if he was trying to hold on for dear life. "Baby!! Oh shit! I'm 'bout to cum. Oh shit...," he said.

When Dirty informed her of that, she continued to suck with her lip pressed with a tight squeezing motion, taking his cum down her throat.

Dirty felt a feeling in his balls and the pressure made him buck and turn to his side where he laid holding his stomach. It was almost as if she had physically sucked part of the life from him and made Dirty feel drained and fatigued. But he knew it was far from being over. Now it was her turn. She positioned herself in the 69 position.

Dirty parted her Garden of Eden, she had a scent that smelled like wild cherry. He licked all on one area on top where the little man in the sail boat hid until Sophelia made him come up for air.

Sophelia was far from being finished with her husband as she spread Dirty's ass-cheeks and with his dick in her mouth, she stuck her finger inside his ass which immediately gave Dirty an exotic orgasm. Ready to explode, his dick was throbbing until Dirty was forced to get up.

"Hey Baby! Let's do it different tonight," she said looking her husband in the eye. As she turned her back to Dirty, never taking her eyes off him, she lowered her chest into the bed with her ass tooted in the air. "C'mon baby! Let me put it in please," Sophelia begged.

Dirty was devastated and confused with what she wanted because never ever would she let Dirty fuck her in the ass.

Dirty looked down between her ass-cheeks. Before she could put it in, he was curious if Sophelia had been tampered with. She took the dick in her ass dry. She opened up like a 7-11 and now Dirty didn't want to think any different.

"C'mon baby. Fuck this ass good," she said.

"Ahh...ahhh....ahhh..ahhhh!" Dirty was in motion pumping the dick in her life, temporarily stopping, the chemistry strange and unordinary as she made faces and threw her ass back like she had been taking the dick like this for awhile.

Dirty figured it didn't take a rocket science to know what was happening with what belonged to him. He didn't want to think the worse.

All of a sudden, they busted-off together and they laid in the bed gazing into each other's eyes.

Dirty explained to Sophelia he wanted her to take a break from her new job training even though it was her career. Dirty had something else he wanted her to do since she had a degree in Sociology.

CHAPTER 8 - COURT ARRAIGNMENT AFTER TWO DAYS

The sheriff called Monica first for the T.V. arraignment with the judge. She came in her orange jumpsuit and stood with her arms behind her back and looked into the camera.

"How do you plea to assault on a female?" the Judge asked.

"Sir, your honor, I didn't have no assault charges, I didn't assault anybody," Monica replied a little confused.

"So, I take it that you plea not guilt, right?"

"Yes, Sir!"

"Let her be released under pre-trial because I don't see any other charges. And next date...."

"Thank you, your Honor!" Monica said happily showing all 32 teeth with a smile that stretched for a mile.

The Deputy Sheriff took Monica out. Then CeCe stood there looking like she was scared when she saw Monica cheesing like hell; she didn't have time to explain what just happened when the Sheriff led CeCe inside the same room.

CeCe was a little jazzy with her mouth, and assured the judge she did not have any altercations with anyone, when the judge asked, "Who's Monica?"

"She just left outta here!"

"You know her?"

"Yes Sir! That's my best friend!"

"Well how do you plea?" the judge asked.

"Not guilty, your Honor!" CeCe replied looking suspicious and didn't know what was next or what the judge's response was going to be.

"I don't see any other pending charges, so I will let you go on pre-trial and set the next court date two weeks from today."

"Thank you, your Honor!" she replied with a smile as if she won a million dollars.

Finally, the women met down on the same floor when they got their clothes and signed out.

One after another, they walked out the door into the lobby. CeCe pulled out the number that Dirty had given them. They had no money to use the phone and no cell phone because it was with their personal belonging. They asked a few people to use their cell phone but still no luck. Then, they saw this guy sitting on a bench in the lobby and he had one.

Monica asked if she could use his phone.

Dude didn't have any problems with that as long as he could get their number.

The phone rang about six times with no voice mail. Monica thought she may have dialed the wrong number. She tried once more but this time a female answered and said. "Hello! How can I help you?"

"Ummm. ...The police officer who gave us this number told us we would be able to get our personal property." Monica said confused and hoping the lady who answered had some answers for them.

"I'll meet you at the front entrance in about 30 minutes; I'm driving a black S.U.V."

"Who are you?" Monica asked.

"I'll explain all that once I get there; okay"

"Wait! What's your name?"

"Sophelia!" And with that, she hung up the phone.

Shortly thereafter, the truck pulled up and they got in. CeCe got in the front seat and looked at this very muscular woman. Then she asked "Where are we going?" She looked at the women and waited for an answer.

"I was told to take you girls to get your belongings."

"Do you know this cop name Dirty?" Monica asked out of curiosity. "Yeah! That muthafucker locked us up and took our damn money," CeCe said being direct and upfront.

"Wait ladies! He got all your shit?"

Sophelia pulled in at I-Hop. Monica and CeCe couldn't figure out what was going on. They went inside, had a seat and got comfortable. The waitress took their orders. Then, about five minutes later, Dirty walked in.

The lady stood up and kissed Dirty and then he sat down beside her.

The New York girls rolled their eyes in disbelief because they thought they would never see him again.

He looked like this was all fun and games. "Em... excuse me, have y'all gotten acquainted, I mean do you ladies know this is my wife? Don't y'all speak all at one time!"

"Where is our fucking money?" CeCe asked with fire in her eyes and a frown that made her look like an 80-year-old woman.

"Baby! You haven't taken them to the penthouse?" Dirty asked like he was trying to shift the weight.

"I was going to do that, but your order was to make sure they were fed," Sophelia replied with a little hostility. She knew nothing about Dirty being a dirty cop. This was something new with the female prostitutes.

Sophelia loved Dirty, she had his back and she wouldn't cross him in any way. Moments after they finished eating, there were questions that need to be answered.

"Why did you have us thinking you were arresting us for drugs and guns?" CeCe asked with her lips press tightly together.

"Because I busted your asses, but yet, I took a liking to you 'Hoes'. That was just a test to see if I could trust you bitches! And I must admit, especially when ya'll felt like a nigga had done you wrong, the frustration that was built inside you two I knew you wanted to see the worst happen to a brother. Regardless how you feel about a nigga, if you bitches are going to make real money. My wife is about to introduce you hoes to some real money instead of walking the streets for a nigga who will cut your throat," Dirty said being serious about the situation.

"Fuck you! I'm not working for you, nigga! Sell my pussy and give you a cut when you can buy some like you done before, muthafucker," Monica said pointing her finger.

Then Dirty said, "Bitch! I'll have your asses locked the fuck up and throw the fucking key away! Is that what you want too, CeCe?"

"No," CeCe said still glad to be out of jail.

"C'mon, Monica! Baby, take CeCe and drop her off at her 'Penthouse while I take Monica back to jail."

"No! Give her another chance please," CeCe pleaded while Monica acted as she didn't give a fuck.

Dirty looked at Monica; her shitty attitude said more than enough. He wanted to kick her in the damn face. Dirty put Monica in the car and then went around and got in.

Dirty thought he couldn't take any chances on this bitch so he traveled the back streets. When he got to a deserted street, he pulled out his gun and stuck it up under her jaw and said, "Bitch, I would've thought you were the smarter one. Not only that, but you also told my wife I paid for pussy; you dumb Bitch!"

Dirty wanted to blow her head through the passenger side window.

Monica dropped tears like a waterfall as the steel of the barrel of his gun pressed hard against her esophagus almost cutting off her air supply.

"Okay," she said as she wept. Monica felt fatigued and exhausted. Blood rushed to her head she felt like she was going to faint.

CHAPTER 9 - THE RIDE

Dirty now had the bitch were he wanted her. He pulled out his dick as Monica held her throat as if it was in pain, and Dirty said. "Bring your ass here, tricks!" Dirty watched as she took his dick and placed it in her mouth, and he said "Apparently you haven't had a real man to control that azz, next time it won't be this good! Your ass will come up missing. Do I make myself clear?"

"Yeah," she said.

Dirty pushed her head back down and headed back toward the 'penthouse'.

Dirty was starting to call his wife to come and get Monica when his phone rang. He looked at his business phone and saw a number he wasn't familiar with. "Hello," Dirty said.

"What's up?" the girl asked.

"Who is this?" Dirty cautiously asked.

"Regina. Remember? I sucked your black Jack off," Regina was a little embarrassed.

"Damn! That's funny because right now I'm getting the real job," Dirty said laughing just a bit as he caressed the back of Monica's head.

"You want me to call you back?" Regina asked sounding different than before when Dirty talked with her last.

"What's your number?"

"The phone booth?"

"Can I come and pick you up? Hold on for a minute"

She could hear Dirty say that's enough.

"Look I'm coming to get you?"

"Okay!"

"Where are you at?"

"At the Food Lion," she said, smirking a little.

"The same Food Lion?"

"Yeah."

"Give me 30 minutes, sweetie."

Dirty finally had gotten an understanding with Monica and the role she needed to play. She had been quietly sitting on the passenger side of the car when she asked, "How did you press charges against me and CeCe without the drugs and gun?" she asked out of curiosity.

"If I give you the game without making the rules, then I'm just a stool pigeon getting his feathers plucked and getting nothing outta of it."

After dropping Monica off, Dirty went to pick up Regina; he thought about how his timing was right and how shit was coming together. Pulling in the parking lot by the phone booth, Regina was nowhere to be seen. Dirty was about to pull off when he noticed she was across the street in front of the tire shop.

"Get in! Can you go with me?" Dirty asked. Looking at her, he thought this woman didn't look nothing like before when he first met her.

Regina told Dirty that her husband, who was a hard-working man, kicked her out when she was on drugs for a two-month ride and she was living with her Aunt and she didn't have any kids.

Dirty threw a proposition out there for her, one that she couldn't refuse. He offered her room and board in exchange for working the streets for him.

Dirty wanted to try the pussy out but he didn't have any time to be mixing business with pleasure right now. Dirty called Sophelia to come to his assistance.

He made it clear if Regina thought she could run off and get high, she would come up missing. Sucking and ass licking is what she was into now.

* * *

DIRTY

Dirty dropped Regina off with Sophelia, who was going to take the girls shopping for some lingerie, while Dirty decided to ride by Pat-Rat's crib now that he had his bitches in check!

He arrived at Countryside Apartments and drove passed Pat-Rat's girlfriend's apartment; he couldn't believe his eyes. Pat-Rat had moved. The blinds were open and you could see straight through the apartment.

Dirty knew they could run, but they couldn't hide. He grabbed his cell phone and called J.J. The phone rang for a minute but no one answered. He couldn't leave a message because J.J. didn't have voice mail. Which, it was a good thing because he knew there wasn't anything nice he had to say.

***

Once at the crib, he noticed that his wife wasn't home yet. Dirty saw there were 3 messages on the home phone. He checked them and the first message said, "Sgt! This is your Drill Sgt. Nah, I'm just kidding," as the Lieutenant laughed. "But seriously, you haven't been answering your cell phone. I was wondering why haven't you yet come back for the new position you were training for? Call me back on my cell phone. Have a blessed day."

Then Dirty listened to the other two messages, all from the same dude. But only the last message said. "C'mon now, I know you probably tired of me calling. Why haven't you called me back yet? Sophelia, call me at home; you know the number."

Dirty was kind of hot for the simple fact dude was calling his house phone sounding as if he was begging for some apparent reason, like it was urgent that he connect with his wife. Even though Dirty knew about the opportunity of her new job proposition, he said, "God Damn!"

Dirty went downstairs to get some quiet time with himself as he opened the safe and grabbed one of the quarter pounds of weed and patiently choked it up. The hydro was the best thing popping, beside pussy.

He grabbed his cell phone and tried calling J.J. on a blocked-number. When someone answered it, Dirty didn't recognize the voice.

"Hello?" the female who answered the phone said.

" I'm sorry! I must have the wrong number. I was expecting a friend of mine to answer his phone," Dirty said certain that the number he had dialed was wrong.

"This is our phone. I'm Justine his girlfriend," she said as she laughed.

J.J. grabbed his phone and said, "Hello! This J.J. What's up?

Click!

Dirty now was laughing because he was sure that was Pat-Rat's old girl. He knew that with just a little time and effort with Justine, he could've fucked her, too.

He tried calling Pat-Rat's phone.

Pat-Rat answered and said, "Yeah? What's up?"

"Look; this me, Dirty."

"What the fuck do you want?" asked Pat-Rat acting like he wasn't afraid of Dirty.

"Pat, I'm calling as a friend. Serious. Listen to what I have to say." Dirty said as he tried to put what he wanted to say in the right context without causing a conflict with Pat-Rat about his bitch. And the worst thing you could do to any nigga is blame his bitch for fucking another nigga; especially when you wanted control of his sensitivity to influence him.

"Where you at?" Dirty asked.

"I just got back into Charlotte. What's up? What do you want?" he asked like he was fed up.

"Call this number but make sure you block your number."

"Why?"

"Look, I'm a friend," Dirty said.

"Whatever!"

CHAPTER 10 - PHONE CALL

"Hello? Who is this?" she said laughing like she was high and coughing at the same time.

"Who is this?"

"Justine! I'm answering my man's phone. Do you want to talk to him?"

Pat-Rat caught the voice and he knew exactly who it was then he heard another voice say, "Hello?"

Pat immediately hung his phone up and called Dirty right back.

"What's up player?" Dirty asked. He wasn't surprised that Pat would call back, but he wasn't for sure that Pat-Rat heard what he heard.

"Where they at?" Pat-Rat asked all hysterical and outta control.

"I don't know. Shit, you know better than I do. I'll ride out with you if you want me to."

"Can you meet me somewhere?"

"Calm down! Where you at right now?"

"Coming through the University, but I'm riding dirty," he said, hyper and intense.

"Meet me at Chili's. Okay?"

Pat-Rat couldn't believe J.J. was fucking his woman and she was laughing and Key-Keying. Right now Pat-Rat wanted to kill this damn cop. He felt like they were handling him and he wasn't going out without a fight, especially for what was his.

Dirty pulled in at the Chili's restaurant. Pat was standing in front of the door. Dirty pulled up in front of the place and Pat jumped in, then Dirty drove around and parked.

"Where's your car?" Dirty asked.

"I'm driving that van over there. Come on, take me to the house. C'mon man. Let's go!" Pat said as his adrenalin pumped like he was raucous and down!

"Where have you been or how long you been away, because they're apparently feeling comfortable with what they're doing." Dirty said trying to get a better understanding before he made a move, not thinking about Pat-Rat's bitch!

"I've been gone for a day. I wasn't supposed to come back until tomorrow. My people met me, that's why I'm back so soon. Now come on, please Dirty. I'll do anything for you, man. I promise you." He pleaded, willing to make some sacrifices with whatever.

"Why can't we drive the van?"

"Listen, Dirty. I've got 60 Kilos in the van."

"Yeh, you're right! We can't drive it."

Dirty kept telling Pat-Rat his girl was not the only girl he was fucking behind dudes' backs. Pat-Rat looked as if he was about to drop tears, as the nigga was a sucker for the woman who apparently had him wrapped around her finger.

By this time Dirty, had finally reached the location where Pat-Rat and Justine had moved to. And just as he thought, J.J.'s car was backed in besides Pat's car.

"Let me out! Stop, Dirty! Where you going man?" Pat asked as he reached for the lock switch.

"Look, calm your ass down! That number you dialed, do you have it in your phone?" Dirty asked him.

"No!"

"Chill out, I'm about to call him and have the nigga meet us somewhere." Dirty released Pat-Rat's shirt from the knot where he had a tight grip.

Dirty called J.J. once again, but this time from his phone. Dirty put his finger up to his lips because he put J.J. on the speaker.

"What's up Dirty?" J.J. asked with so much joy in his voice like he knew that he'd hit a gold mine.

"What's up nigga? What you doing?"

"Boy, I'm getting my head waxed! She something terrible, too. But what's up?"

"Damn! That head job is like that?"

Then they heard Justine say in the back ground loud enough to hear, "You mad it's not yours!"

That was it. Pat folded up in his seat holding his gut. Dirty convinced J.J. to meet him in about 30 minute at their favorite spot, then hung up.

"I can't believe this bitch, playing me like that. Man, I'll kill this bitch!" Pat-Rat kept coherent but he looked pitiful.

Dirty pulled in where he and J.J. normally meet. Then, Dirty reached under his seat and handed the gun back to Pat-Rat.

"Why you giving me this?" Pat-Rat asked looking at Dirty like he was very confused turning the gun over in his palm.

"It's yours! Shit, she's fucking and sucking. Kill his ass. No exceptions! Don't go pussy now!" Dirty said rubbing the matter in deeper. Then Dirty told him he had his back.

J.J. had just pulled in and Pat-Rat lay back in the passenger seat. He cocked his tool. J.J. got out of his car walking towards where Pat-Rat was sitting.

"Damn! He's coming to your side. Hold up there's a car passing by." Then Dirty quickly got out and said, "Come here and show a nigga some love!" Dirty walked back behind the rear of his car and gave J.J. a thug hug.

J.J. was a little older than Dirty. He had been with the Police Department for almost 9 years. J.J. was divorced for cheating with his wife's sister. He was 5'11", wore a low haircut with waves circling his whole head, and was built like a Pit Bull. But he was selfish, arrogant and greedy.

"What's up Dirty? This had to be important because nigga, I left my bitch for this conversation." J.J. kept bragging about a bitch that didn't belong to him.

Pat-Rat was curled up in the floor of the passenger side of Dirty's car, tired of listening to this muthafucker bragging about how he molested his bitch. Pat-Rat opened the car door when Dirty and J.J. turned to look when Pat came up the side of the car and busted off three shots, hitting J.J. in the head once and the body twice.

"Get the fuck in the car Pat-Rat!" Dirty screamed grabbing J.J.'s cell phone while he dragged J.J.'s body out of the way from where Dirty had to back the car out.

They left the scene and J.J.'s body lying on the ground, dead as hell. Pat sat there crying like a little bitch. Dirty thought how all this was over a damn woman who had Pat-Rat twisted.

"Put that gun in the towel and wrap it up," Dirty said.

Dirty put the gun under his seat and then drove Pat back to Chili's. Dirty parked beside the van. For a moment it was silent as Dirty thought heavily about their next move. He had the evidence on Pat that determined whether he died of lethal injection or the gas chamber for killing a cop. Dirty knew he was just as much to the blame.

"Hey Pat! He's dead, man! He's dead! He ain't coming back. You best believe there is going to be a lot of heat coming down in the Queen City for killing an off-duty Cop. This is what I need for you to do, are you listening to me?"

"Yes, sir," Pat replied as if he were delirious.

"You aren't supposed to come back to town until tomorrow night?"

"Yeah"

"Check in at a Hilton Hotel across the street on W.T. Harris, and stay there until tomorrow. If your girl calls you, answer the phone and act as if nothing ever happened. Do not question Justine. Just love her like you never had before. You got that?" Dirty asked as he gazed into Pat's eyes and thought how he would kill 'em if he had too.

"What about the drugs?" Pat asked.

"Follow me and I will transfer the dope to somewhere safe." Then, they drove to a nearby car wash, pulled inside and took the drugs out of the van and put them into Dirty's car. After that, Pat-Rat drove off in the van.

CHAPTER 11 - BUSINESS

Sophelia and the girls were now just coming back from the shopping spree. CeCe, Monica, and Regina had all shopped for lingerie, Sophelia had total control over the escort service, and she knew exactly what men wanted and how they wanted it.

Sophelia was associated with a lot of white and black men more than anyone could possibly ever imagine and she figured being in this line of work they had to be hand-picked carefully and needed to be both optimistic and clever, and were willing to pay for pleasure. Everything she ever did was up to her expertise and never would she settle for less than whatever was needed to do things right.

Sophelia thought about how Dirty had convinced her that tomorrow was just a dream, not unless you contest the competition and the rival, and come off the wall fighting for what you believe in. And Sophelia felt as if she had done that well as Technical Sergeant.

They now were getting accustomed to their 'penthouse'. CeCe and Monica were taking a liking to Regina. She explained to them her weakness and addiction that effected her marriage and why she's in this situation to cause her life to be so unstable and vulnerable.

"Shit, look at it this way girl. You don't have to worry about that flunky nigga anymore; that's the reason why me and Monica are down here behind a tired-ass man beating and dragging us. Now we can get a wet ass and get paid for it, and enjoy life to the fullest," CeCe said meaning every word that came out her mouth.

"Shit! I'll be real about the whole shit, because when I thought less of Dirty, him being a cop, and how he handled us at the beginning, I hated that muthafucker! Especially how he did us downtown had me feeling like life was over. His dirty ass brought us off the streets from walking in the cold long nights," Monica said.

"Yeah! Alright, you already told Sophelia you fucked her man, bitch. So, you better love the one who is paying you to lay between your legs," CeCe replied being sarcastic and picking on Monica.

"Girl! He did pay!" Monica said looking sure about what she had just said.

"Sophelia is the bitch in charge, and she's the one who is making future preparations and appointments to get us money. Girl, just sit back and enjoy the common-wealth while Sophelia governs this event," CeCe said.

The girls had more than enough room. The penthouse was staked out in mostly red material, a couch, a polar bear white carpet; no shoes were allowed, a 63-inch plasma T.V., a two-way mirror and a nice Jacuzzi with enough room for five people.

They took CeCe's advice and cuddled around their domain.

***

NEXT DAY AT THE POLICE PRECINCT

The Chief of Police had the floor. All the officers sat quietly and were eager to hear what he had to say. Dirty sat in the front row giving his undivided attention.

"Ladies and Gentlemen, as you know a bad tragedy has occurred with one of our fellow colleagues was found dead yesterday. There wasn't any sign that he had been robbed but the body was moved.

After the Chief said what he had to say, everyone was supposed to keep their ears and eyes open for anything that might help them get a lead in solving the case. You best believe they weren't stopping until they did.

Dirty felt like if it was his life that was lost, he would expect for them to do the same thing.

Dirty went to the bathroom and dashed some water on his face before he walked inside the office of his Chief of Police.

Dirty was at the door and took a deep breath before he would enter the office. Then he knocked.

"Come on in!" the Chief yelled.

"Carlos, have a seat, son. How can I help you? '

"Look, Chief, I just talked to J.J. yesterday, and now he has popped up dead. How, I mean, he was fine; like nothing was bothering him. If he did have a problem, I'm pretty sure he would've told me," Carlos said acting out his role as a concern friend.

"So. ...Emm. ...Carlos, I'm sorry. It's just J.J.'s murder, and the personal problems I'm dealing with are almost like a snow storm. Emm. ...Look, son, just keep your ears and eyes open because you could be the next victim. Once upon a time, I controlled the streets. I want you to come down harder in the 'Valley' and ask questions; be careful."

"Yes, sir. I will Chief." Dirty said as he got up and excused himself from the office.

Dirty jumped into his police car and left the parking lot. He grabbed his cell and called Pat-Rat.

"Hello?" said Pat-Rat, sounding like he was just getting up.

"What's up? I need for you to check out and meet me for lunch at I-Hop in 30 minutes," Dirty said.

"Is it safe?"

"Calm your ass down! Everything is fine, so far!" Then click.

Dirty thought about the 60 Kilos he had in his possession, and how many of them belonged to J.J. who no longer mattered. Dirty thought he got what he deserved for trying to step on his toes.

Dirty pulled in at the I-Hop and had a change of mind because he had on his cop uniform, and that wouldn't look right.

(DISPATCH)

"We have and emergency on 49 Hwy; a man is about to jump to his death."

"COPY," Dirty replied.

Dirty picked up his cell and called Pat-Rat and told him he had an emergency call, and they would have to meet later.

Dirty arrived at the scene. There, on top of a building, was a skinny, white man around. ...Maybe 25 to 30 years old. Dirty thought this shit was crazy. He stood beside another officer and said, "What's the problem? Why is that dude on top of the building?" Dirty asked.

"He lost his job," the cop told Dirty.

Dirty couldn't believe how this character had all these people out here watching his bullshit. Even the fire truck now was trying to set up a ladder.

"Jump, muthafucker! You're wasting my time. I've got business to be conducting. If I was behind your ass, I'd push you to your death," Dirty was pointing a finger trying to catch eye contact with the victim.

Finally, the wife shows up and yelled to the man on the top of the building. "Either you jump, Bobby, or climb down now. You hear me Bobby? You stupid ass! You're not going to jump. You are dumb," she screamed.

As the police grabbed her she yelled out that he walked away over a fucking job and his ass needed to jump.

The police had Bobby apprehended. Dirty helped clear the area and finally after two hours, everyone was gone.

Dirty called Pat-Rat and asked where he was at. He was still right where Dirty asked him to be – at the car wash. Dirty thought how today was beautiful; the sun was shining and the flowers were blooming and the leaves on the trees were pretty

Dirty figured one more lick and he was set for while.

Dirty pulled in at the car wash, and spotted the white van sitting in the cut. He pulled beside it as Pat-Rat sat there. He rolled the window down. Dirty knew he had Pat-Rat by the balls.

"How many of them belong to J.J.?" Dirty asked. He just wanted to hear the response.

"Nah, I pay cash money for this. J.J. didn't kick in a penny." Pat-Rat said. He went on to say, "J.J.'s cut was 37%."

Dirty thought J.J. was being robbed; 37% ain't shit.

Dirty thought half was good for him, but he would rather have the money that Pat-Rat gave to his supplier to buy the dope. He thought about what he would give to get at the Big Man. First, Dirty had to see where Pat-Rat's mind was before he could even trust this nigga. Dirty couldn't afford for Pat to share it with his bitch. Justine was a diva; she voiced out her demands on the phone. Dirty right now couldn't let whatever Justine was doing with her mouth to these niggas have an influence on them.

"Look! You're doing big things and I'm going to continue to embrace you on that. But you took a cops life; you understand me? The heat is going to continue to come down. I trusted you before and you went behind by back. Shit, how do I know you won't do me the same way again?" Dirty asked as he looked Pat-Rat in the eyes to see what kind of response he would get.

"Dirty, you got me dead to the right. I don't want to go to prison for the rest of my life. I promise you that. I'm in it too deep to turn around. I've got your back; I will give you whatever you want. I have a couple of million."

Dirty's dick got hard and stood up; he had Dirty's attention. Dirty didn't want to over react, because he had a position to play. Then Dirty said to himself who in the fuck is this nigga? For real, why isn't Pat-Rat connected with support? Normally a hood nigga wouldn't worry about not having protection, but Pat-Rat wasn't built like that; Dirty knew the hood would eat him alive.

Thinking is what Dirty did best and he told Pat-Rat, "I need for you to check back in a hotel somewhere!"

"I told Justine that I was on my way back," Pat-Rat replied like he missed her dearly.

"Look, I've got to protect you as well as myself, dude. Do you understand? It's important for us to keep a low profile, because we would make the CNN News, man. Can you promise me if I do decided to let you go there, you won't tell your girl shit? Act as if you just got back."

"Alright!"

"Later"

CHAPTER 12 - HOME

Dirty changed clothes.

Sophelia was on the computer scouting for clients. Dirty kissed her on the lips but she turned her head and rejected him.

Time was pushing; he had to meet Pat-Rat.

Dirty left, driving his ninety-thousand dollar truck, and headed to Matthew, NC where he agreed to give the dope to Pat-Rat. Dirty knew his wife, she played a tough girl role. Never had Dirty been in a situation where he had another woman admit to his wife right there in front of them that he fucked her. Dirty thought he would worry about that later on down the road.

It was about 10:00pm when Dirty finally pulled in the park. Pat-Rat hadn't shown up yet. He sat there for about 15 minutes before Pat pulled in driving a white van.

Watching for any sign of anyone, Nobody. Pat walked around where they were face to face with each other. "Look Pat, you got to be careful driving back up the hwy at this time of night"

"I'm straight," Pat replied.

Dirty popped his trunk as Pat opened the Van and they quickly passed the dope to the car five at a time. Dirty thought this nigga was trafficking a lot of shit to be a man on his own. Dirty thought how something wasn't adding up right. He watched that dude pull the trigger and he didn't care nothing about why he did it.

This bitch was someone special, Dirty thought. She was a working woman that wanted something out of life and was getting it the best way that she could. Pussy doesn't do a nigga like that, especially the way he was acting and all those millions of dollars he claimed he had. A bitch could be brought by the dollar.

Dirty's conscience teased him now to the point that this little nigga showed he didn't care about the law. So what made him think he cared anything about Dirty?

After Dirty and Pat-Rat finished loading, Pat left; they decided to chop it up on the phone.

They left the park and got back on the highway, Dirty trailed almost 50 yards behind Pat. His phone rang. "Yeah," Dirty said.

"Look, Dirty; are you alright with me? I did some shit the other day, kinda outta of my mind, and you didn't bother to look at me any different after I went behind your back to get you fucked up! You're strictly a 'get money type dude'. This shit is probably far from being over, but I want you to know, my mouth is sealed."

"I'm straight! It's your mouth you better protect!"

"Shit, I never liked the nigga - period."

"But how are we going to work out the finances? What do you suggest?"

"Keep your mouth closed and soon I'll make you a millionaire. There is one thing that I need for you to do though."

"What's that, player?" Dirty asked as he thought how the dude was finally coming to his senses.

"It's this nigga that owes me for eight kilos and then said fuck me. I could've touched the nigga, but I don't want blood on my hands. Since you work for me, and me working for you; fuck them. Shit, I want the nigga off the street. Killing him is too good of an award. I want him to sweat every day behind bars jacking his dick while I write a love letter telling the nigga how I'm fucking his bitch." Pat-Rat said.

"Shit. Blood didn't stop you from killing a cop!"

"That's different! That pig had his dick in my girl's mouth."

"What's so important about this bitch? Is there a chance she might flip on your ass because you couldn't keep your mouth closed?" Dirty asked waiting on any hint that might help him figure out this puzzle.

"I've got to stay in my lane, Bro. That's all I'm going to tell you." Click!

Dirty felt like he was holding this nigga's nuts up for him to cum. He thought he had shit in control, but what the fuck? His mind was on those millions!

Dirty had a lot of thinking to do so he decided to head home to chill for a bit and try to patch things up with his wife. He thought how tomorrow was like a million miles away. Until then, a nigga like him had to play his position, and participate in the moment.

Dirty showed up, and to his luck, Sophelia was gone. He didn't want to worry about what his wife was doing with the bitches, because Dirty knew she would handle her business. Sophelia wasn't the type of woman that liked to be followed up on. He then went down downstairs and settled in for a moment, rolling up his blunt as his mind drifted. Then all of a sudden, Dirty heard a buzz for the door. He pushed the button and he heard Sophelia walk in downstairs.

"You need anything? I didn't have any intentions of cooking," she hollered up at him.

"Nah, I'm straight. But thank you for telling me you aren't gonna cook," Dirty replied.

"I'm on the computer handling some business; that's the reason I didn't cook shit. I agreed to help you out," Sophelia said as she headed upstairs.

CHAPTER 14 - DIFFERENCES

Sophelia was on the computer with an old friend who was planning on paying her a visit with the escort service that she now had rolling. Sophelia dealt with all the finances and sent the clients to the addresses without supervision because Monica and CeCe were real professionals.

Sophelia couldn't stand to be around Monica after she admitted fucking her husband to her face; she wanted to take her ass out. But she knew it was all good. They were straight hoes that strolled the streets.

Then Sophelia received an e-mail from 'Flex' one of the guys that was stationed at Fort Bragg in Fayetteville, NC. He was an old friend of Sophelia's and he was on his way to Charlotte for business and a fuck. So Sophelia hooked 'Flex' up with Monica for $800.

Monica would just have to hold her breath; hopefully she'd pass out and die.

OPEN HOUSE

There was a knock at the door and when CeCe answered it, there stood a man about 6'8" inches tall weighing about 415 pounds. He was blacker than the night outside with perfect white teeth and a nice trimmed haircut; he was somewhat handsome looking.

The man asked, "Monica?"

"Come in. Umm...what's your name?" CeCe asked as the dude made her look like an ant.

"Big Flex."

"You can have a seat. Can I get you something to drink?"

"Yeah, Monica," he said with a smile that was attractive and warm, as he was just a big country Teddy Bear.

CeCe disappeared around the corner. Once she got to Monica's room, she knocked twice because Monica was still asleep. "Girl!! Get yourself together; you have a visitor waiting on you," CeCe said smiling and anxious to see the expression on Monica's face when she saw who Sophelia had hooked her up with.

"How does he look, CeCe?" she asked rushing and making preparations. She didn't want to hold her client up. She knew looks had nothing to do with business.

"Bye girl, I'll keep him company until you come"

"How do he look?! Shit, I know you heard me, Bitch!" Monica busted out saying.

"Damn! He's cute, now hurry-up and bring your ass!"

CeCe was in the kitchen when she screamed out. "You sure you don't want nothing to drink?"

"Yeah I'm sure; I've got to drive. That and alcohol don't mix for me. I really am a firm believer against drinking and driving."

Finally, Monica came strolling through the living room with a warm embracing smile that welcomed the big guy. She was moved to the point where it was impossible for her to change her facial expression because of what she had seen.

Big Flex stood on his feet and was amazed at how beautiful Monica was.

She approached and grabbed his hands and guided him back.

"Hold up, Big Flex! Please…" Monica said with her legs bent up under Flex's armpits, were he laid his heavy weight against her body leaving her breathless and in pain. She grunted with each stroke of his 12 inches that touched the inside of her stomach.

"Hold please?" Monica cried with the uncomfortable feeling as if he was just grudge fucking her.

"What's wrong Baby?" Big Flex asked sweating and dropping all his body fluid in her face and over her breasts.

"Let me ride it, I can ride it like I'm robbing a bank," She tried to bribe him.

"But this is the position I paid for, Monica. I thought it was supposed to be about customer satisfaction, or I'm going to have to request a refund?" Big Flex asked.

'No. Baby you don't have to do that," Monica said as she rubbed her toes on the side of his face. She was now soaked.

"That's it. …Right there, Big Flex!!!"

"Shit!" Monica exclaimed feeling he was in her stomach. "Yeah. …Oh God. Shit. Ahhh. …ahh. …ahh. …ahh… ahhh…"

Big Flex rotated his ass cheeks as he sped up making music as his odor roaming into the air, pushing into Monica's nostrils. She couldn't believe the funk on this big, funky-azz nigga.

After a few hours of no strings attached, Monica didn't walk him to the door. She dried up sweat that was piercing her skin.

CeCe bumped into Flex walking up the hall which was a no-no. Customers never see themselves out.

"That Bitch tripping! I was about to ask for a refund," Big Flex said.

"How come?" CeCe asked. Her facial expression changed when she thought that Monica could jeopardize the type of easy money that they were making instead of them strolling the streets like real working hoes.

"Look I'm sorry. Is there anything that I can do to make your stay better?" CeCe asked trying to be courteous to the customer.

"Nah! I'm straight. But next time, I want somebody different." he said as he walked out the door closing it behind him.

"Yo, Monica? Where the hell are you?" CeCe screamed, mad because they both knew how Dirty could be notorious when Monica was already on his hate list.

Then, CeCe thought about how long Regina had been in the room with her client. When she realized Monica was in the shower, CeCe knowing they had to look out for each other, knocked on Regina's door. Then she knocked a few more times, thinking the dick couldn't be that good.

When the door came open just a little bit, then Regina peeped out and said, "What's up?" She looked like she was in a tangle.

"Damn, you trying to spend the night, ain't you?"

"We're about finished."

"You're using protection, right?"

"Yeah!"

CeCe let Regina finish up; then there was another knock at the door. CeCe quickly ran to the door and answered it.

"I'm Cedric. I'm looking for Monica."

"Emm. Come in please; you can have a seat in here. Just give me a minute. Can I get you something to drink?"

"No. Just Monica," dude said laughing.

Damn, CeCe thought as she walked away. What the fuck?

CHAPTER 15 - NEXT DAY

Dirty's wife was lying in the bed when Dirty left the house without kissing her; something he had not ever done in their eight years of marriage.

It was 5:30 a.m. when Dirty pulled his cruiser out of the garage trying not to draw attention.

Dirty left, heading to the precinct; he knew the tension was going to be floating around in the air especially when there was a dead cop and no leads.

Dirty clocked in, but was eager to get outta there. Then, he spotted the Chief. It was only right for Dirty to pay respect and honor to his fellow officer and assure the Chief he was doing everything in his authority to bring the suspects to justice.

The Chief, far from being stupid, wanted Dirty to crack down on the gangs in the Hidden Valley area.

Dirty left the precinct driving down East Way heading to the location he seen his jay-walkers. He pulled on Timmbrook and drove down in the cul-de-sac, he parked in the circle and watched a couple of people leave the apartment walking up the street, apparently leaving their car behind. Then, someone came out of the apartment and sat on their porch. The guy looked like he had done nothing wrong. Dirty sat there watching for about 45 minutes.

Pulling away, Dirty thought how he would be back before they knew it, but right now his main concern was to go jack niggas asses up and shake up some brothers for no apparent reason.

Dirty's phone rang. When he looked, it was Pat-Rat. "Scar. What's up"" Dirty asked.

"You remember what we talked about, right, dude?"

"Other than that, what's up?" Dirty asked. He got the address from Pat-Rat. Dirty knew he was going to get his share of his money from him. Dirty hung up.

***

A nigga they called Kelly-Boy moved from Macon, GA. Dirty had seen him from time to time driving a four thousand dollar car that was sitting on 29 inch rims. Kelly-Boy most definitely was not liked by Pat-Rat.

Dirty drove through by Kelly-Boy's crib. He wasn't there but the trap boyz who he fucked with were. The guys from the Valley protected Kelly, meaning niggas were ready to go to war with this nigga on any given day.

Dirty pulled Kelly-Boy's photo up on the computer. He had a bald head, dark skin with long braids coming from his chin; all of his teeth were gold.

Dirty thought the area was infested with crack-head roaches, trying to bring the community down slowly but surely. He pulled up behind two cars that blocked the street, grilling Dirty as he went by. The youngsters were quick to shoot at the law. Even through the community was like a little city of its own, Dirty thought if they tried him like that, regardless how much they hide in the Valley, they will come out sooner or later.

Dirty liked it when he did things on his own, but right now he had to call his snitch up, (Monkey Wrench) Cory who pretended to be a part of the drug game but used more then he sold.

"Hey Dirty? Talk to your boy," Cory said needing some powder.

"You know this nigga named Kelly-Boy, don't you?"

"Who don't?"

"I need his whole routine. You know what I'm talking about?"

"Shit!! I need money, my girl's check hasn't gotten here yet."

"What good are you to me broke? Your ass needs to be in jail with the rest of the roach-eating ass niggas that can't make bail."

"Yeah, alright. Bye" Click.

Dirty headed home early. When he pulled up, he saw Sophelia talking to a man in their drive-way. There was a chemistry that looked as if they had been attached before.

CHAPTER 16 - PAT RAT

Pat-Rat sat in silence, patiently waiting for his source to show up.

When Justine came in the living room, she said, "Why the fuck are you so quite? You know what, I can't stand it when you get in your bitch-ass ways, Rat!" she said grilling him from the side of her eyes.

"Ain't nothing bitch about me OLD HO!" Pat said defending his manhood.

"You're not even worth it, Pat-Rat!"

Three men approached the front door and knocked.

Pat-Rat opened the door and shook Justine's father's hand. Justine came running towards her father and said, "Hey, Daddy! What are you doing here?" Justine looked at Pat-Rat and tried to figure out what was going on.

"To be honest, I'm about to find out myself," Speedy replied. Speedy was impatient and had a low tolerance when it came to dealing with his "Yeya" (cocaine).

Speedy was from Rowann County but he lived in Statesville, just outside of Charlotte. Speedy supplied over five states and was tied to the Mob.

'Okay, I'm listening. What's going on?" Speedy said as Justine looked puzzled and confused. She didn't have the slightest idea what Pat-Rat had to talk about.

"Well, we have a cop who is extorting niggas." Pat-Rat said as he hesitated for a moment.

"I'm sorry, Mr. Speedy! But the reason I called you is because of this cop I killed," Pat said, now dropping his head, looking down to the floor with his hands crossing each other.

Justine was surprised that Pat had killed J.J. after she had gone behind his back and fucked him.

He went on to explain how J.J. came into the picture after Carlos.

"If J.J. was going to be some kinda protection for you, from Carlos, why did you kill him?" Speedy asked, knowing this was deep.

"Justine!"

"Justine?" Speedy asked.

"I don't even know what lies he's talking about Daddy; for real," she said with a serious look on her face with her eyes wide open like she couldn't believe this shit. Now she was eager to see what the fuck Rat was talking about. She knew it was impossible for him to know shit when he was supposed to be out of town, so she thought there was no-way in the hell she was going to tell on herself.

"Look, apparently we're not going to get to the bottom of this if you don't say what you mean!" Speedy said.

"Justine, you fucked your brother," Pat said looking at her like he despised her ass.

Justine looked as if she had to hold her breath, before she could respond, or tried and defend herself.

Speedy tried to explain to Rat that he had a high-level connection in the Charlotte Police Department.

"Look Pat! I'm connected with some people here in the Charlotte area!" Speedy said looking him directly in the eyes.

"Speedy, the cop still has the gun I used to kill the officer. Please! I beg you let me handle this, sir." Pat said looking distinguished from the others.

"Son, I don't know what you have in mind, but this is business and not personal. I know you probably could back some of it, but what happens when it becomes a problem you're not able to pay?"

Speedy look at Pat-Rat like he wanted to ensure the young man that it is very serious killing a cop.

"It's not going to drag for that long sir; just give me some time for now and I promise your money will be exact." Pat said as he looked Speedy directly in the eye.

"Okay son! I guess I'm done here. Take care of my daughter; if you can't do anything with her, please send her back home to Daddy," Speedy said as they got up. Speedy walked to the door with his arm around Justine.

Justine and Pat-Rat watched as Speedy pulled out of the drive way. They waved, then walked back inside the house.

"How you figure that I was fucking J.J., Rat? Huh? Tell me, please. I want to know my damn self?" she asked waiting for Rat to respond.

"Bitch! One reason is your ass is too simple. You think I'm a lame, right?" Pat asked looking like he wanted to beat her ass, pointing his finger in her face.

"So, I'm a bitch now. You haven't seen shit! Move your finger outta my face!" she said aggressively. "You know this is your world, I'm just a squirrel trying to get a nut and getting shit on in some form or fashion."

Pat went in the bedroom and thought how tired he was.

CHAPTER 17 - DRIVE WAY

"Hey, Honey! Ummm... this is Lieutenant Brown. He paid me a visit to see why I haven't returned to work. He claimed that he left two voice messages on the phone," Sophelia said.

"Matter of fact, he did. I'm sorry I didn't tell you, but he acted as if he was horny!" Dirty said looking Brown in the eyes like he couldn't fool him.

"Excuse me, Mr. Bowmen!" Brown replied changing his facial expression with his chest bowed out.

"Hold please!" Sophelia extended both arms across their chest.

"You better be lucky," Dirty stated.

"Or else, or else what? You going to shoot me?"

"Yeah! You said it. But you're lucky. I said before my job is to protect and serve. Sophelia, get your company out of my damn yard." Dirty said walking away.

Then you could hear Sophelia say, "Just go, please. I'll call you later about the job."

Sophelia went inside the house and Dirty was already downstairs in the basement, when he heard the buzzing sound, but didn't want to be bothered. Dirty put his wife on the loudspeaker and asked, "What's up?"

"Can we please talk?" Sophelia said talking through the intercom.

"Talk, I'm listening."

"You are my damn husband and I refuse to talk through some fucking intercom. If you can't be a man and stand on the situation, then I'm out."

Dirty thought she needed to take her shit with her. For a moment, nothing was said—just silence. Dirty could hear her breathing through the intercom. Then Dirty could hear the echo of the door being slammed.

Dirty pushed the code in on the computer and checked the accomplishments that they had established. The account showed $21,000.00. "Damn, them hoes been doing some fucking," Dirty said out loud.

He made some calls informing his police task squad that they had a bust lined up for the next couple days. Dirty had his informants putting in work trying to see what his best objective would be. Dirty strolled through looking for 'Kelly-Boy' to see what his real name was, but he couldn't find anything here in Charlotte. No warrants for this particular address. Dirty kept strolling through the computer, still nothing. Then Dirty decided to call Pat-Rat.

"Hello," Pat-Rat said answering his phone.

"Yo! What's the business?" Dirty asked as the other end got quite for a moment.

"I've got 75gs for you right now, but before you get that, have you taken care of what I asked you to?" he said then waited for an answer.

"It's going down this week and that's for certain." Pat said and then hung up - Click.

He thought if Pat-Rat had just done what he wanted. And now, hanging up on Dirty, it's like he'd already forgotten that he killed a cop. The nigga's acting like he doesn't have any worries at all. Dirty was going to have this nigga come up missing.

* * *

PENTHOUSE

"Damn, my fucking abs are sore as hell," Monica screamed.

"All that fucking, big pussy, as you would say. You must of run into a horse dick," CeCe said and started laughing.

"Bitch, fuck you! Today is our day off. What's up with some drinks uptown?"

"I don't care. Let's see if Regina wants to come."

Knock, knock, knock. Monica kept knocking as she yelled, "Open the door."

It took almost three minutes for Regina to open the door. "What's up?" she asked with her eyes wide like she was scared or something.

"You wanna ride with us uptown to get something to drink? Hey, first of all, what's wrong?"

"Nothing. I just got off the phone with my husband. I'm good. Y'all go ahead."

"You sure?"

"Yeah!"

Monica and CeCe left the house and Regina had called a new friend she had met while sleeping with a client, which was one of the rules that was prohibited. But this was one of her off days, and she would do what she wanted, at least that's what she thought.

There was a knock on the door and Regina answered it. Sophelia walked right in and went to the kitchen table like she normally does when she paid the girls. Regina went to the back and immediately tried to call her friend when there was another knock on the door.

Sophelia jumped up and went to the door to answer it. "Chade! Why are you here? I don't remember setting an appointment up for you." Sophelia said as she looked puzzled.

When Chade put both hands up, his hands said it all – he didn't know.

Chade was one of Sophelia's soldiers who she mostly dealt with as business for the girls.

Then Regina came back in the living room and heard what was going on, and she said, "Here are your eye glasses," as she handed them to him then put her hands on her hips.

"Oh! Okay. Okay that's why you told me to come back," Chade said lying through his teeth.

"First of all, you guys are not to have each other's number or have any communication. Regina, what's really going on?"

"Look, Sergeant! I apologize. I really took a liking to her and asked for her number."

"If you like her that much, you will continue to see her through our network. Make sure this doesn't happen again."

They said their goodbyes and he left.

Regina really liked Chade, but Sophelia told her there are going to be plenty more studs that will come through her life that she will like. She will get over this one.

CHAPTER 18 - NEXT DAY

Dirty drove down Snow White Lane in the Hidden Valley area at about 8:30 in the morning. Dirty thought he would drive by Kelly-Boy's trap house. When he approached Bilmark, Kelly-Boy's car was backed in beside the house. Dirty kept on driving and decided to call his little monkey wrench (Corey) when all of a sudden. ...

"Hello," Corey said.

"Where you at?" Dirty asked him.

"I'm just leaving from dropping my wife off at her job, what up?"

"Yo! You're fucking up. Don't make me lock your ass up! Damn it."

"Why? What did I do, Dirty?"

"What the fuck *haven't* you done is the question, dumb-ass nigga."

Dirty had Corey's attention and they came to an understanding. Not only that, but Corey decided to use his own money to get the job done.

Dirty drove the neighborhood, which was like a maze. He came up where there were crack-heads running away from a car that just pulled off. When he did, Dirty trailed, riding the bumper of the other car, making sure they didn't throw anything out the window.

Dirty looked at them making unnecessary moves inside the car and they looked through the rear view mirror giving themselves away.

When they thought it was safe, Dirty dropped back just a little being hesitant when he turned on the lights pulling up full force ahead as he rode their bumper until the guys pulled over.

Dirty sat there for a minute. The guys in the car freaked.

"What are we going to do with this gun?" one dude said to the other.

"Shut the fuck up! He didn't have any reason to pull us over anyway."

"Oh shit! Here he comes. Damn, I'm not holding this gun."

"Wait. When I say throw it out the window, do it," the one dude said sweating from his forehead.

When Dirty approached the car, he walked to the driver's side and carefully looked inside the car.

"Yes sir, officer." the driver said.

"Why were y'all in a drug area?"

"No officer! That was my cousin," the passenger side dude said.

"I tell you what! Since you muthafuckers want to lie, get y'all stinky asses out the car and cuff up," Dirty said.

Dirty sat there listening and at the same time laughing. Then he said, "You know what happened to the last muthafucker I took the cuffs off of, huh? Bitch muthafucker, do you really want to know?" Dirty asked looking at the suspect through the plastic window.

"Yeah, I know what happened to him. You probably sucked his dick, pussy-ass Cop," as the one dude spit on the plastic window.

Dirty opened the back door and punched dude twice in the face, "Suck this, bitch!!"

The dude spit on Dirty again and thought to himself, that's just another charge – a helluva one, at that!

CHAPTER 19 - COREY

Corey pulled up at Kelly-Boy's trap house, got out and knocked on the door. One of Kelly-Boy's answered the door.

"What's up Corey? Come in, man. Who you wanna see, Kelly-Boy?" the worker said just getting up.

There was one other nigga laying on the floor and two on the couch in the living room.

Corey looked around and saw a digit scale on top of the kitchen table, paraphernalia everywhere.

Kelly-Boy walked in. "Yeah! Ummmmm. ...What's up, partner?" Kelly-Boy said as he cleaned sleep from the corner of his eyes.

"Kelly-Boy! I need two ounces of hard, but it depends on what you're charging," Corey said looking at Kelly like what little money he had was his last and that the product was for him.

"Ummm...damn, boy! I ain't gonna lie. It's hard around here; it's dry as hell. It's hard to find some dope."

Then Corey thought how all drug dealers sell their drugs like it's their last fare from being dried when the City was flooded with anything you wanted.

"Damn Kelly-Boy, don't do that. My man got dope but I fuck with you, shit. ...I'd rather see you with it," Corey said smiling just a little trying to get himself a lesser price.

"That's what I'm talking about there, partner. Boy, you know this is Kelly-Boy; I'm from GA. I done seen it all, but since I fuck with you, I will let you get each one for $800; a piece, that's it."

"Alright!"

"Swig! Go get that out the bathroom, and weigh him out two of them things."

Kelly-Boy wasn't stupid; he kept the dope in the bathroom in case he needed to flush it. When Swig returned he handed the bag to Kelly. Then one of his hood-bitches came from the back and said, "What's up, Baby?"

"I need fifty dollars."

"Here, I'll see you later." Kelly looked into her eyes with one of those thug smiles he has.

The young girl left and Corey said, "Shit! I see why you charge a nigga an arm and leg."

"Hell, yeah! My bitches are like my cars. ...they need gas, too. If not, them hoes will not run. That there, I can't afford for them to stop doing partner."

"You must not talk to Red anymore." Corey said.

"Shit, I don't see why. She's at the crib where we live. You think I would fuck my wife up in some shit like this?"

"You did her?"

"C'mon Dawg! I'm a player pimp, them my ghetto chicks, that's all! Don't you got a bitch you wouldn't never bring around your job?"

"Yeah – my wife!"

"Alright then."

Finally after about an hour and a half, Corey was about to ride out, when he stopped on the front porch everybody now was wide awake and traffic was starting to pick up.

Corey left heading home when he picked up his cell and called Dirty.

Dirty picked up on the first ring. "Damn! It's about time. What's up monkey wrench?"

"What? Tell me what the fuck that is supposed to mean?" Corey asked.

"I was just fucking with you, Nigga! Tell me something good."

"Look! Dirty there's about four niggas in the house and not only that, if you plan on getting the work, you better bring your own because Kelly-Boy ain't stupid. His dope is setting right beside the commode in the bathroom."

"Do you know how long Kelly-Boy going to be there?"

"Yeah, he's not leaving until about 6:00 this afternoon. Why do you ask?"

"Because I'm thinking about hitting the house now," Dirty said. Normally he wouldn't tell his snitch anything because just like he snitched for Dirty, he would go behind his back and do the same for someone else.

"C'mon that would be stupid! Shit that would look like I set that up!"

"You scared, bitch! Huh? What's wrong with your little Rat ass?"

"Dirty! Dirty. ...C'mon man, don't play me like that, this here is real, this is my life! I'm helping you out," Corey said dealing in his feelings.

"Nah! You're helping your damn self! You want to stay out of jail. You was in the wrong for breaking the fucking law!"

"I didn't break shit! Your ass set me the fuck up!"

"You want me to lock your ass back up?"

"C'mon Dirty!"

"Straighten your ass up then you little bitch!"

Click! He hung up.

CHAPTER 20 - 3 HOURS LATER

The water meter man walked along the neighborhood, now on Bilmark Street just five houses away from Kelly-Boy's trap house. He grabbed his walkie talkie and said, "Dirty, do you copy?"

"Yeah, loud and clear!"

"We have two people sitting on the porch and one is at the edge of the drive-way talking on a cell phone."

"Does it look like he's got a ponytail hanging from his chin?"

"Yeah, a long one."

"Right. When you get to the house, give me another call."

"10-4."

Dirty and six task force men were on the other street waiting to make a move. The only thing that Dirty could think about was the 75g's that Pat-Rat had waiting for him once he had Kelly-Boy behind bars. Dirty thought it would've been easier to just kill the nigga. Then the thought kept running in Dirty's head that J.J. didn't do anything that he wouldn't have done, but never in a life time did Dirty ever think he'd would've run into a package that was bigger than life itself, and what it had to offer him.

"Dirty, do you copy?"

"Go ahead, meteorologist," Dirty said laughing.

"Well, it's partly cloudy and I'm here right now as we speak, standing over the water hole."

"Okay, turn it off. We are on our way! Did Kelly-Boy go back inside the house?"

"10-4!"

Dirty trailed the task force squad as they turned on Bilmark and cars pulled up to the residential area pulling all over the lawn as two tried running off the porch where the officer that checked the water pulled his gun. The two stopped in their tracks and fell to the ground. Inside the house Kelly-Boy laid there on the floor of the hallway with two officers that had him apprehended with his arms behind his back and one officer had his knee stuck in Kelly-Boy's neck.

In the bathroom, Dirty pulled out the dope from inside the commode that Kelly-Boy tried to flush. There were about 40 bags that wouldn't flush down the toilet. In the shower were 18 ounces; half were crack and the other half were soft, powder cocaine. Like Pat-Rat said, enough to put Kelly-Boy away for the duration.

They seized about ten grand, just a small fraction of what Kelly-Boy kept on him at any time.

Dirty whispered inside Kelly-Boy's ear, "Pat-Rat said that's your bitch is what he wants." Then he put Kelly-Boy in the back seat of the police car.

Kelly stared at Dirty like this shit was unbelievable. Kelly knew there were two ways to skin a cat and the money and dope he still had was a shot caller of its own.

They put the rest of the suspects inside the van as Dirty drove off with Kelly-Boy, separated from his crew.

"Yo, Kelly-Boy. Where the fuck you get a name like that from? Shit sound country as hell," Dirty said with a smirk.

"I got it from your mommy!"

"Damn…what's up with all the mommy jokes? Oh yeah, look, I'm not gonna ever stoop to your level dawg."

"Yeah….that's right dawg, that's the type of name we use around here, Kelly-Boy! You country muthafucker!"

"You tell Pat-Rat I'll kill his ass," Kelly said.

"I told that stupid muthafucker we should have just killed your ass instead of sending you to prison and give you an opportunity to still jack your dick."

"What do you mean, 'we'? Huh, you son-bitch," Kelly said trying to get answers from the cop that appeared to be dirty.

"Why did you take the man's dope and not pay him? You know he wants your bitch?"

"Pat-Rat will never get my Bitch. She loves me, partner!" Kelly-Boy said.

"C'mon Kelly-Boy. She'll move on to the next dealer to support her. Why is that so hard for you to understand? Don't be stupid," Dirty said.

Dirty pulled into the intake. Kelly-Boy made it clear he didn't care for working for the cops. Fuck'em as Kelly would say.

After all was said and done, Dirty knew his job was to throw away the key.

CHAPTER 21 - MEAN WHILE

"Ahh...ahh...ahhh....ummmm... that's it Lieutenant hit this ass, unh...unh.. shit! drill me...you fucking...jar-head," Sophelia said with her head pressed against the wall and her neck bent, her ass up in the air and her back arched with a curve in it as Lieutenant pressed hard in the middle of her lower back.

"You fucking don't want to follow orders do you?" Lieutenant said as he kept sliding his dick in and out of Sophelia's ass.

"I'm sorry...oh God!...that's it," Sophelia pushed back as she squeezed her ass-cheeks back onto Lieutenant's eight inches. He sweated hard all over her back, and ass.

"Turn your ass over girl! That's a fucking order. Right now!" As Sophelia turned and positioned herself, never taking her eyes off Lieutenant as the sweat from his body was turning her on.

Lieutenantgrabbed her legs while Sophelia braced herself with both elbows flat pressed on the bed mattress. He placed each chocolate long muscular leg over his shoulder as Lieutenant watched her smooth skin and between her thighs her pussy lips partially laid opening as Lieutenant rubbed the head of his dick in between Sophelia's wet pussy that was throbbing for the dick her husband refused to give to her. She couldn't believe the thickness of his dick was wider then her wrist. His dick opened her up wider than she could probably go.

Lieutenant had Sophelia in where he laid tightly pressed against her with thighs touching each side of her ears.

"Ahh..ahh...ahh..." she moaned, as Lieutenant had Sophelia in a position where she was unable to move putting all his back muscles into it that followed each rotation.

The Lieutenant's dick was covered with cream of Sophelia's love juice as he kept pumping the dick in and out of her without a rubber with the sensation that they both felt enjoying the unprotected sex.

"Oh...God!!!! Take it out, Lieutenant. You're about to cum. I see it in your face ...please, please! Don't cum in me," Sophelia begged, helpless and not able to twist out the lock position. Then he had her jacked what he had in his little sensitive balls as he grunted with sensation that felt phenomenal. Then he placed his sweated face up against her when he kissed the side of her arm, the one she used to dry his face off.

Sophelia got up and jumped in the Jacuzzi as she relaxed her mind trying to get some dignity about herself subconsciously.

She knew she couldn't blame Dirty when she started from the beginning fucking her Lieutenant Sophelia knew she couldn't stay there long because she had business to run, and now she was starting to love it.

* * *

HOME

Dirty had been home now for almost four hours and not a sign of his wife. He was now skeptical about the woman he thought he loved.

Finally as Dirty sat there in the living room, he watched his wife as she tried straightening her hair when she exited the vehicle, still pulling on her clothes as if she felt like she was out of whack, when Dirty realized he saw exactly what he was looking for with her deceiving ass.

Dirty walked down stairs to the basement before she could come inside the house and thought nothing she did surprised him at all anymore. Maybe, he thought, Monica was the fault, but Sophelia had shown other symptoms about herself. He knew for a fact that she had changed; like her wanting to be fucked in her ass. Dirty thought how he had a freak for a wife, but she had to go away from home to get dick inside of her stinking ass when Dirty felt like she could've got it from him.

He felt like maybe he might have needed to move on instead of letting this beat him up mentally.

Dirty now had fired up a blunt and exhaled as he took a deep breath and blew out the feeling that made him feel somewhat fatigued. His world no longer felt complete without the woman he'd promised to love for the rest of his life. He knew he should get himself as far away from his wife as possible without coming between his hoes and business they had established together.

Dirty grabbed the cell phone and called Pat-Rat.

"Hello!" the female voice said.

Before Dirty decided to call out a name, he thought before calling someone else that he really didn't know who it was, and said, "Ummm... is Pat there?"

"Who is this?" Justine asked."

Dirty almost started to say, ain't you tired of answering people's phone, but now he saw that was just a regular routine for her.

"Dirty!"

"Don't I know you?" She asked as she kept coherent trying to see if the name rung a bell.

Dirty heard Pat-Rat in the back-ground say, "Who is it?"

Justine said, "Somebody name Dirty."

Then Dirty heard, "Tell 'em I'm not here."

"Hmm...Dirty I thought he was still outside, you want me to tell him to call you back?" Justine asked.

Then Dirty thought this nigga wanted to play games so he said, "Alright, Justine!"

"How you know my name?"

"We smoked a joint together at your crib when you lived in Country Side Apartments, remember?" Dirty said sweating the memories of the moment when he held her hand.

"Yeah! I thought I knew you! hey...." Click!

Dirty started to laugh because Pat-Rat wasn't trying to let super-head get loose.

CHAPTER 22 - WORK

Dirty grabbed the gun he had gotten from his bitches, the little .38 pistol. He placed it in his back pocket in case he had to blow a hole in Pat-Rat's head for not paying him his money.

Dirty pulled in at the Food Lion parking lot and decided to pull up Kelly-Boy on his computer screen to see what was his real name and the statistics he was looking for. "Bob Stub" outta Macon, GA was now out of Mecklenburg Co. jail on bond.

"Damn!" Dirty thought how this nigga knew something; especially when they gather handguns. He just knew that it was over for Kelly-Boy.

(911 DISPATCH)

"There's been a disturbance, possible assault on a female on Allen St, off Parkwood Drive."

"Copy! I'm on my way"

Dirty thought he knew this particular address and when he pulled up, just like he thought, he did. It was Corey his monkey wrench.

Dirty parked and got out. He looked at Corey and pointed for him to bring his ass over to him.

Corey must have been drinking because he gave Dirty the middle finger. Dirty walked in his direction now only 10 yards away as they stood almost face to face when Dirty said, "Nigga, why are you out here acting stupid in my streets? Have you lost your mind?" Dirty looked him over because never had he seen this type of attitude before. And Dirty became cautious and didn't know what to expect.

"Nah! I haven't lost shit muthafucker! You think I'm a damn Monkey Wrench! I heard your muthafucking ass the other day bitch!"

By this time four other police cars pulled up and got out and one of the officers asked Dirty, "What's going on?"

"The suspect said that he was going to kill me! I don't know what he got on him; I never been able to get close because he had the advantage to pull before me," Dirty said lying out of his mouth.

All the cops drew on Corey. "Get your ass on the ground, now! Right fucking now!" They all yelled at once.

Corey dove to the ground face first. They had him twisted like a wash cloth.

They threw Corey in the back seat of a police car and drove off, leaving Dirty behind.

Dirty said to himself, "Don't that muthafucker know not to communicate any threats on a police officer of the law? How dumb can he be?"

One thing about Dirty; he didn't want a snitch for too long. Especially when he knew the snitch could just as easily confide into someone else as they did him.

He drove off heading to the other side of town were Pat-Rat now was living temporarily. Dirty thought how he was going to start putting more pressure on Pat because now Dirty was working him, but still hadn't gained shit from what he'd already done.

Dirty pulled up at the car wash, backed up into one of the stalls, and grabbed one of his cell phones and dialed Pat.

"What's up?" Pat said.

"Where you at?"

"I'm home! Why? What's up?"

That's the shit Dirty was talking about right there. Dirty thought how this nigga was starting to smell himself.

"You got my money?" Dirty had asked.

"So, did you put "That" in jail?"

"Where else is he supposed to be? In the ground?" He said, now a little upset and frustrated, ready to kill this nigga.

"Where the fuck you at pig!? You trying to handle me?" Pat-Rat asked.

Dirty was looking devious and ready to explode at any moment.

Moments later Pat-Rat pulled into another stall beside the one Dirty was parked in.

Pat walked to the truck with a brown bag that contained the money that he owed Dirty.

Dirty grabbed the bag and quickly unwrapped it and couldn't believe his eyes; he was satisfied with the accomplishment.

"You know, I thought I told you to stay far away from my woman Dirty?"

"Look here in my eyes you stupid muthafucker, because everything I'm about to tell you is real. I don't know who the fuck you take me for or what the fuck you are trying because it won't work. You better respect me muthafucker! I'm the fucking law you dick-head son-of-bitch! Fuck your bitch! Now get the fuck out my truck!"

"Okay officer, I mean Mr. Officer, you take care and protect and serve," Pat-Rat said opening the car door and slamming it shut. Walking away never taking his eyes off Dirty.

Dirty pulled off and decided he would clock out a little earlier than he anticipated. Driving home he thought how his wife must be sick and tired of him. Dirty knew there was nothing that he wouldn't do for her. He just wanted to be alone and as far away from his wife as possible; just the thought that she was sleeping with another man was enough for him to pack his shit and leave.

He pulled into the driveway and saw that Sophelia's truck was parked in the yard.

Dirty grabbed his bag and walked to the door, but before he could reach it the door came open and there stood his wife looking as beautiful as the first day he ever laid eyes on her.

"Can we talk please?" Sophelia looked as if she had lost her best friend in the world.

"Give me a second of or two while I take this bag downstairs, and I'll be back."

Dirty returned and Sophelia sat at the dining room table with all ten fingers caressing each other.

Dirty sat down and didn't really have anything to say besides the business that he already considered letting Sophelia have since she done a good job with the operation.

"It's really been a long day, and I'm really not up to talking right now. But I can be a good ear for you." Dirty said looking into the blue, avoiding looking at his wife.

Sophelia didn't want to hear that; she got up and walked off.

CHAPTER 23 - TWO DAYS LATER

Dirty left the house feeling good. He had slept in the basement where he had been for the last past couple of days. He decided to pay the girls a surprise visit. From his understanding today was a pussy rest day.

He smoked a blunt on the way over and was feeling pretty high when the door came open; it was Regina who answered the door.

Dirty walked in before Regina could tell him no. Closing door behind him she had on a see-through night grown without any panties on. Dirty had a seat in the living room and couldn't help but stare at her.

"What's up Dirty?" Regina said as she sat down crossing her legs looking totally different from the last time Dirty had seen her. Her toe nails were done and she wore her hair in a pony tail. You could see her nipples just as clear as day and when she noticed Dirty looking, she crossed her arms, showing a little decency. Regina knew she was already naked, but she was home.

"Ain't shit!" Dirty said, "I just needed someone to talk to about my marriage and the shit that's being troubling me, that's all. But before we get into my personal life, how have you been doing and where are the other girls?" Dirty asked, like he was concerned; he was really just being noisy.

"You are supposed to be in court with them today right?" she asked, looking for a response.

"Oh yeah, yeah! They will throw those charges out, but what's up Regina?"

"Nothing! I just got off the phone talking with my Aunt and she said I was much better off leaving my husband where he is, and just go forward. She believes he would use that same excuse to fault me for other things besides me getting high."

"What do you mean use the same excuse to fault you? Damn, you missing me with that one." Dirty said a little confused to where Regina was trying to go with what she was saying.

"In other words, he would use an excuse to do what he wants, when he wants too."

"Okay, okay, I feel what you saying now. That's true, because I'm a man and any excuse is better than none."

Regina got to the point where she was relaxed talking to Dirty. He had an excellent view of some perfect jugs with nipples that looked if they needed to be licked.

After a moment Regina asked Dirty if he wanted something to drink. Of course Dirty said yeah. She got up and immediately Dirty's dick got hard. Regina had the roundest ass, and the crack of her ass-cheeks folded, rubbing together as Dirty watched her turn the corner.

"Damn!" Dirty thought, watching Regina return. The view of her pussy lips had aroused him, something no man could resist. Apparently she was aware that she enticed Dirty in a lot of ways.

"Here you go," she said, handing Dirty the water bottle. Regina was as close as he thought she would ever get. Dirty reached out, wrapping his hands all the way around her thighs and put the bottle down on the floor. He laid his head up against the side of her legs and gripped her ass-cheeks and massaged them as if he wanted to cherish something that didn't really belong to him.

Regina stood and as Dirty had his way she placed her hand on the side of his face, never seeing this side of him before. As he got more emotional with the gentle touch, she could remember her husband had once done that.

"Dirty, what's wrong?" Regina asked, as she grabbed for his chin and held his face up in the air and tried as hard as she could to gaze in his eyes. But Dirty refused to reveal that part of his sensitivity.

Quickly Dirty stumbled to his feet and rushed for the door. Regina grabbed for his arm but Dirty never turned around and walked out the door.

Dirty now was in a position where every second of the day haunted him mentally. J.J. was dead and his Chief wasn't stupid. And Dirty almost forgot about his duties as a cop to harass niggas for nothing.

Blacks are the targets for any event that occurred. Because Dirty thought that black people were so in denial about their own people making a change that it had sunk so far into their system that they didn't care. He knew sooner or later that something had to be done or the finger was going to follow Dirty and point at him.

Dirty didn't know if his monkey wrench had gotten out of jail as of yet, but he needed to talk with Corey. Dirty drove to that part of town and parked at the check cashing spot. He reached for his cell and dialed Corey's number.

"Yeah! Corey, I apologize for what happened; don't worry I'll have all charges dropped against you, but there's a favor I need from you real bad."

"What the fuck you want!?"

"I need Kelly-Boy's phone number; I need to pay him a visit."

"You think he'll want to talk with you after you done busted him with all that shit! You'll tell him that you got the number from me. Hell NO!!!"

"Quit tripping scared-ass nigga! Let me get that number."

"Yeah it's going to cost you!"

"What! Anything, what's up?" Dirty asked, wasting no time when he needed to get at Kelly-Boy.

"I need some money bad, somebody peeped my stash"

Dirty cut Corey off and asked him for the number. When Corey refused until Dirty gave him the money, Dirty convinced him to meet him in the cut were they sometimes go to talk.

Dirty backed up in the cut, and waited for him to walk through the path like he normally would do. Then Dirty peeped him coming up through the woods.

"What's up Dirty?"

"Let me get that so I can go!"

"You got me right?" Corey asked with the little shit-eating grin he had on his face.

"Yeah where's the number?"

"Here!" Corey handed the number to Dirty on a piece of paper and Dirty reached on the floor and grabbed the .38 that was already cocked.

"Here you go you snitching ass bitch!" Pow! Pow! Pow! Pow!

Dirty quickly opened the door and grabbed the shells that almost burned his hands.

Corey lay there, lifeless, with a nice size hole in his head and three others to his chest; he never seen it coming.

CHAPTER 24 - DAY AFTER THE SHOOTING

Dirty was exhausted but never lost sleep behind his killing. Niggas were forgetting who Carlos was. There were some niggas that walked that path and found Corey's body a few hours after he had been shot.

Carlos went on with his daily routine; he had more business to take care of. But his wife was his number one priority. He only seen her once in two day's since being off. He had to go to work tomorrow so he planned to nip his problem in the bud today.

Dirty wanted to be relaxed with some of the decisions that he had made; he had almost a quarter of a million and wasn't yet finished with what he wanted to establish.

He sprayed in the basement to kill the smell of the marijuana scent that hung in the air.

After locking everything up, and checking behind himself to lock the door, he walked into the den where Sophelia sat at the computer getting her money in. She seemed to be content with her hair wrapped up and one foot jacked in the chair that she sat in. She communicated with friends, truly the ones she probably done fucked, Dirty thought to himself, thinking he knew the woman he was in love with, and had married.

"Sophelia, if it's possible can I please have a talk with you?" He asked high as hell and wanting to fuck - but not his wife.

"I'm busy right now; what about later Carlos?"

"Yeah, alright!" He walked away, and thought how she played her little games going from one activity to another. Dirty could admit one thing about his wife; when she takes charge there is nothing he can say to get her undivided attention.

Dirty decided that he would go out and enjoy the rest of the day; he had to be back to work tomorrow.

He wanted to finish something he'd started with Regina, but he knew it was impossible because Sophelia worked them like the call girls that they were. The games that Sophelia enjoying doing, especially the communication she was having with the soldiers, she probably actually had some involvement with them.

Dirty pulled up at a bar on South Blvd - a little pool room called, "Yellow Rosa's". He parked and looked around before getting out of his truck. Once inside, Dirty noticed the women just sitting around chatting. Some of them were playing pool. Dirty ordered a double shot of tequila and placed some salt between his thumb and index finger. He took the shot to the head then licked the salt off his hand. Already he felt the alcohol that had him feeling so good. Any more, he thought, and he would be scared of himself.

Dirty turned around and directly in front of him was Justine chillin' with two other girls. He turned back around not wanting her to see him; as bad as he wanted some pussy, he knew that she was a freak. Dirty didn't want to fuck his money up for the near future with her man. Then again, he thought, a quick nut wouldn't last forever, just the feeling each might fall victim to the pleasure of joy. "Shit! Then a nigga out," he said to himself.

Dirty ordered another double, and thought it would be best if he'd just get the fuck outta Dodge, when all of a sudden some little fingers touched him on his shoulder. When Dirty turned already scared of who it might be, and to his luck: "Hey! hmmmm....Carlo's - is that it?," Justine asked.

"Yeah!" he said, thinking to himself, 'I was afraid you'd remember.'

Dirty looked Justine in her eyes, and knew right away what she wanted to do. She was so beautiful to be so easy; you could smell the alcohol on her breath and right then she didn't know fucking with Dirty that he was a mad man.

"I haven't heard from you since Pat-Rat hung up on you. What was all that about?" She waited for an answer.

Dirty didn't know how much she really knew.

"Shit, to be honest, I really couldn't tell you; I thought me, and dude was alright," he said.

Justine turned toward her girls and said to them with a hand signal that she'll be back. Then she took him by the hand and lead him to the outside.

Dirty said, "Where are we going? It has kinda done got late, it's dark outside."

"Where's your truck?"

"Right over there"

They both climbed into the truck. Dirty thought now this shit was crazy and, before he could set in the seat good, she had already unbuttoned his pants and grabbed his dick. He thought there wasn't no way in hell she could take all his dick.

"What the fuck! How long is it?" She asked as she adjusted the dick in her hands. Then she placed it in her mouth, and just sucked like a true head hunter.

Dirty put his hand on top of her head and enjoyed the blow job when he went back in memories about something she had said about a muthafucker being jealous 'cause he couldn't get his dick sucked. And now she had a mouth full of his dick. Dirty could no longer take the blow job because he felt he was about to explode. Quickly he took his dick out of her mouth, and made her turn around with her arms rested up on the back of the seat and reached grabbing her jeans from the side and pulling until he had them below her ass-cheeks. Her ass, from the back, was amazing. Dirty posted up behind her without a rubber on and rubbed his dick head that was throbbing and pushed into her wet pussy. He used little strokes, because she was that tight, until she finally had gotten loose when she start saying, "Ahh...Ahhh...Ahhhh...Ahhhhh ...stop Carlos! You're hurting me!" She felt the dick inside of her stomach touching her in places that felt so good. She pushed her ass back onto the dick as her wetness surrounded it to perfection.

Dirty pumped faster and faster when he was about to nutt he quickly withdrew and nutted on her ass. Dirty was so backed up that Justine felt the warm cum splash down her back. Dirty kept pulling until he had all of it out his dick. He was still hard as he watched Justine's pretty ass but there wasn't enough time for to go one more round.

Dirty reached in his arm rest and grabbed a cloth and cleaned her butt cheeks. Then he put her out of the truck and left her standing there in the parking lot as he drove away blowing the horn.

CHAPTER 25 - HOME

Dirty had just left Yellow Rosa's after fucking Pat-Rat's woman and he thought was *that* worth risking Gigs? The pussy was like that, tight and he could now understand why Pat was like he was about this freaky-ass bitch.

Finally pulling in the driveway Dirty sat there for a moment listening to power 98, it was dark going on 12:30 a.m. at night. He could see Sophelia walking back and forward in the house as if she was talking on the phone. Then all at once she came out side with some of her workout shorts on.

She walked up to the window and Dirty rolled it down just far enough to hear what she had to say.

"Yeah! What's up?" Dirty said, looking crazy.

"Open the door on the other side please," Sophelia asked walking to the passenger side.

"Unlock the door Carlos!"

Dirty got out locking the doors behind him; with the inside smelling like pussy. He refused to go out like that.

"What's up?" Dirty said as he kept walking toward the house.

"I'm trying to talk to you! But you keep on walking away."

"Look! I'm tired, I been to the bar and I'm drunk and I have to work in the morning let's do this tomorrow.

"Whatever man! Sophelia said stopping on the porch and sitting down on the steps, trying to figured out what she wanted to do with this illegal prostitution ring and continue to enhance and better her career so she was able to prosper and make better preparations for their son.

Dirty got out of the shower and dried off, looking in the mirror and thought about how everything looked good on the outside, but there were more problems of his own that he was scared to face or deal with, so he wanted to overlook it as a thought of being.

Surely this was a mistake if Dirty thought he could lay in his bed and rest, but took his chances without smoking a blunt fully aware of his expectations and intentions. He rolled over relaxed and drifted just a bit when Dirty felt his wife's arm hug across him as she threw her leg on his hip like she always done and whispered in her husband's ear and said. "It's going to have to be some changes Carlos, just listen to me please! You may hear me and you may not.

* * *

TRAPPING

"Hey, hey! What the fuck I tell you junkies! You think I'ma keep looking out for you leaving your post? You let the Police pull up on me I'ma skin your ass partner!" Here! Now get your ass back down the street.

Kelly-Boy wanted to get at Pat-Rat so bad when it was impossible because he didn't have the slightest idea where to start.

Back at the trap house, the same routine; less sleep and more paper chasing. Kelly thought he was a fool the first time, he done got so relaxed and the money was coming so good Kelly started sleeping were his gold mine was. He made a helluva change within himself; he was out on bond and really couldn't trust nobody any further then he could see them.

Kelly-Boy left the trap walking down the street on the other side where his car was parked and his nigga "Swig" was left in charge. Kelly-Boy was on his way home to "Red" his main bitch, who Pat-Rat once met and fell all the way in love with.

Pulling out of the Valley Kelly-Boy headed to his townhouse.

Like the cop said to Kelly-Boy, he was lucky to be here and if it was up to him he would be dead.

The game had become a lot more serious, but it's a blessing Kelly's still here to talk about it. And he knew they wasn't done and what Kelly refused to do was run from a bitch nigga who had put the cops all in his business.

There were two things for certain: Kelly-Boy didn't want to change the location, especially when money was flowing like a waterfall, and every dollar meant more to accumulate, it's better than Jay-z, when he said. "I sell water to a whale." *That's* tight.

Kelly-Boy went inside the townhouse and peeped in the master bedroom. There she was laying on top of the sheets with nothing on, barely looking as if she had ever been touched before in her life. Her skin didn't have a scar or stretch mark. She lay on her stomach like a gift from God, her ass-cheeks were beautiful and her back was narrow. The muscles in her legs were from jogging every morning. When Kelly would be coming in the house she would be leaving. She had long hair and looked like Stacey Dash. She was fully developed and very much mature. She was any man's dream and surely Kelly-Boy wasn't ready to give up on her.

CHAPTER 26 - BACK TO WORK CONFERENCE ROOM

"Listen Carlos it's not looking good! Still you haven't come up with the slightest clue as of yet with J.J.'s murder! I'm really starting to worry son," the Chief said, concerned about another Cop death.

"I'm on a lead right now Chief! I'm just waiting on an informer to get back with me this afternoon sir!" Dirty said, lying and realizing how important this was and knowing it wasn't a game anymore. Time was limited and what Dirty needed was someone to blame.

Now Dirty was ready to leave the office. Because he had heard more than what he expected, he wished he had just kept his damn mouth completely shut instead of telling the Chief he was last seen with J.J.

Leaving the precinct Dirty grabbed his cell phone and called someone who probably didn't want to talk to him. The phone rang on and on with no answer.

(911 DISPATCH)

"We have an emergency 911 call in the North Charlotte area on Allen Street. It's believed to be a pregnant woman who has been stabbed in the stomach; suspect is to believe to be the mother's boyfriend. He's wearing blue shorts and a wife beater; still believe to be on the scene."

"Copy! I'm on the way"

"Fuck! Fuck! Fuck! Damn-it, fuck! Who in their right fucking mind would stab a woman that's carrying baby?" Dirty said as he rushed to that part of town as quickly as he could; he had a million thoughts running through his mind of problems of his own.

When Dirty showed up there were patrol cars and a fire truck, and Ambulances that had arrived, which was good for him. There was no telling what he would've done to the suspect that sat there in the back seat of the police car if there were no witnesses.

"What happened? Besides dude stabbing her, what was the reason to justify such act?" Dirty questioned one of the officers that was doing some paper work. The officer pulled up his belt on each side like he had a heavy load of ordinance.

"The crazy muthafucker stabbed his girlfriend, because she told him the baby wasn't his. Then she told one of the paramedics she was just playing with him because she said he had cheated on her," the officer explained to Carlos.

"That still wasn't a cause for him to stab the woman and possibly cause both of them to lose their lives; what kinda condition is she in?"

"The knife missed the baby's head only about an inch."

"How far along is she?"

"Eight months, she's gonna be alright. They're gonna watch her at the hospital, and maybe force her to have the baby, if there are complications. Somebody's bill is gonna be sky high!"

"Thank you!" Dirty said, patting the officer on the shoulder as he walked toward the patrol car where the suspect was sitting in the back seat. He had no shirt on and was looking down as if he was ashamed to look up.

The suspect wasn't anyone that Dirty knew; and he thought he knew everybody from the North Charlotte area. This was only two blocks from where he had killed Corey.

Time had gotten the best of Carlos and it was already time for him to get off. So he left there and headed home.

When he pulled up in the yard Sophelia's vehicle was parked. He went inside closing the door behind him.

Sophelia still had her leg up in the chair wining and dining the computer like there was no better place she wanted to be. And this is where Dirty left her, passing to go downstairs to transfer out of his police uniform into something comfortable.

After about five minutes, Sophelia came to the door and tried to buzz in. Dirty was funny and turned on the loud speaker.

"Yeah, what's up?" Dirty asked through the loud speaker.

"Is this how you want to talk Big Guy? Well if that's the case then! I did cheat on you with Lieutenant Brown!" Sophelia replied as she looked down at the floor from where she stood.

Sophelia could hear the breathing through the speaker. Dirty had gotten very sentimental at the disappointing news; something he had already known, but hadn't been confirmed until now. His voice dragged and he was once again alone in his mother apartment with roaches running all over the place and her in the other room having sex to support her drug habit. He thought Sophelia had loved him. She was everything a man could want in a woman, but the thought of her sharing herself with another was just too much to bear, and it crushed the past and present memories of their togetherness. The loud speaker went completely off as if he pulled all cords.

Dirty grabbed his bottle of Hennessy and drank heavily, fighting the anxiety of dealing with what he was now feeling inside that was now dead.

Picking up the phone, Dirty had called Kelly-Boy.

"Yeah! Who in the hell is this?" Kelly-Boy said as the number showed up 'unknown'.

"Dirty!"

CHAPTER 27 - "HOT SPOT" NEXT DAY

"Hey, hey, don't park your azz right there! Take that ole hot ass car further down the street," Kelly-Boy yelled out looking for the Cops both ways.

"Man quit tripping! The crack-head replied"

"Tripping? Tripping my ass! You be at every drug house in the city, keep ridding partner," Kelly pointed down the street for the car to keep moving.

Everybody was riding in the Valley. You had certain niggas that lived in Hidden Valley taxing other drug dealers because they ran a particular zone. That's why Kelly-Boy had gotten acquainted with the so-called killer who dared for a nigga to cross his path.

"Hey Swig! Man....come here! You know we better than that!" Kelly-Boy said.

"What?!"

"Send them crack-heads on down the street, we gettin' too hot!"

"They Fam! Kelly-Boy"

"Fam, hell! Send their asses on farther down the street instead of in front of the trap house! C'mon Swig, we closing down here in a few, we got some business to conduct now."

Kelly was thinking how this bitch-ass nigga put the cops on him. If he was real nigga, then he would've come back and claimed what was his. Being half bitch and half snitch, put the two words together, what you got was a fearless drag queen who didn't want a real nigga to know what was under his dress.

Inside the house on the kitchen table was a couple Glocks, and an Ak-47 power rifle. Time had passed and it was now dark. Kelly backed the S.U.V up to the back fence and loaded the guns; they had all the artillery they needed to shoot up a police precinct.

Kelly-Boy drove while Swig sat on the passenger side. Closing the trap house down Kelly-Boy pulled out and headed to Pat-Rat's crib.

"Hey Swig! You ready to do this, huh?"

"Hell, yeah! How did you find out where this bitch lived?" he asked, looking as if this business here was personal.

Finally, driving past the crib, Kelly-Boy seen Pat-Rat's car parked. On the side of the house was another car he didn't recognize.

Kelly said, "Hey! Look here now, I don't know who might be inside the house, but we gonna be ready in case somebody got to die! You heard me! Huh?"

"Yeah! I got you Kelly-Boy"

"Look here, hey! I'm not used to this shit, you hear?"

Kelly-Boy looked with both eyes opened; skeptical about the whole ordeal, but this was something that Kelly had to handle.

"Don't worry! I done it before," Swig said with a smile on his face like he was excited about it.

"Nah! Look here! We ain't kicking in no door period! Understand me? We'll knock first, and if that doesn't work, you can kick the house down."

Swig had a small body frame weighing 178 pounds and he wore his pants off his ass, with braids in his head. Finally they parked in the drive-way and got out of the truck, Kelly stuck his Glock magnum in his back while Swig grabbed the Ak-47 and rested on the side of the house. The community wasn't in a bad part of town; it was 8:30 p.m.

Kelly walked up on the porch and knocked; Justine opened the door and said, "Who is it?"

Swig ran from the side of the house as Kelly-Boy stepped back giving him enough room to run Justine over. Kelly took his hand gun, and put it in Justine's face as her eyes looked like they were about to pop out of her head.

Kelly closed the door behind him; they worked like professionals, almost like they'd done this before.

When your life depends on something like this, automatically your performance enhances to your best ability, and the other Party actually is stung. They are so afraid that they are hoping the gunman will spare them their life and just praying they could possibly be blessed with one more day of life.

Finally as Kelly-Boy walked Justine into the bedroom, there he was, Pat-Rat on the floor butt ass naked, Swig had the barrel of the AK stuck in his neck.

"Turn his ass around Swig! Yeah, this way. Leave 'em on his knees, yeah, face me you pussy ass snitch! Muthafucker you told the cops on me!'

"No I didn't!"

"Yeah you did, yeah you did!" Kelly-Boy smiled showing all his 32 gold teeth.

Justine sat there in the corner of the bedroom with her face turned toward the wall like she was positioning herself for a "time out".

"Where the work at?" Kelly-Boy asked while Swig pressed the barrel of the rifle harder into Pat's neck.

"It's under the house!" He replied not wasting any time telling him.

CHAPTER 28 - CLOSE BY

(911 DISPATCH)

"We have a 911 emergency call on the North Side off North Tryon Rd. On Green St 405, victim has been shot, and it's possible that the victim is living"

"Copy! I'm on the way."

Dirty drove pushing the gas pedal to the floor. His mind raced because he knew exactly who stayed at this particular address. When he arrived the ambulance was already there. He parked and was sitting there in the car watching the set-up when he saw Justine crying her eyes out. Dirty grabbed his hat and put it on, trying to disguise his identity.

Dirty grabbed the plastic bag with the gun inside that Pat-Rat had used to kill J.J. They now were wrapping the house with yellow "crime scene" tape to secure the possibility of any evidence that they were able to use, because Pat-Rat was dead.

Dirty walked around like the other cops looking for any forensic evidence. When he finally got alone in the bedroom he quickly dumped the weapon under the bed kicking it as far as it would go. He knew they would find it when they got around to doing a thorough search for this investigation. Dirty eased his way out of the bedroom, trying to hurry up to get out of the house.

When Justine had to go back inside the house to grab her pocketbook, she ran into Dirty.

"Oh my God! You! Hey you"! Justine said as she got a good look at Dirty's face.

"Yes mum?" Dirty replied, acting like a complete stranger, but professional and concerned about a matter that he thought she may have.

"I know you! You mean to tell me you a Cop!?" Justine said. Now crying and realizing that this shit was a puzzle that she had almost figured out. This damn cop was the other cop that Pat-Rat had been talking about. It had to be, but she wasn't quite sure. She had tears rolling down her face, and gazed Dirty in his eyes, and said, "This shit is far from being over! You hear me you dirty azz cop? Let me find out you had something to do with this!" She said in a low voice like she really meant business.

Dirty pushed the young lady to the side because she was acting delusional, and confused about what she just said. time was limited until the gun would be discovered and he didn't want to be there on the scene whenever it was found.

Dirty got into his cruiser and as he pulled out he seen Justine watching as he disappeared down the street. Dirty's heart was beating rapidly, and he thought how he wished he could've somehow ducked and dodged Justine.

It was now 11:00 p.m. - time for Dirty to get off work. He went home and changed clothes as well as vehicles and left, heading to the car wash.

There in the back of the car stalls was parked a truck that he had seen Kelly-Boy driving before.

Dirty pulled up beside Kelly-Boy and said, "Why you let the bitch live?" Dirty was frowning and highly upset. While they talked, Swig transferred half of the 48 kilos that was left into Dirty's truck.

"Fuck you! She wasn't my problem! I got Pat-Rat's bitch ass! My nigga shot him in the head. Now what about the charges you promised to take care of for me?" Kelly-Boy asked.

"That's gonna cost you!"

"What?! I looked out for you!" Kelly said like he was mad."

"You looked out for your damn self!" Dirty replied with a greedy look that said he wanted it all.

"I just gave you 25 of them things, two more than me, and you ain't done shit, you dirty muthafucker."

"Fifteen more of that you have now, will take care the charges." Dirty said with greed written all over his face, wanting all he could get.

"Leaving me with 8 kilos huh!?" Kelly said. He could easy put a bullet in between Dirty's eyes, but right now he needed them charges taken care of. His "Red Bone" bitch is all Kelly could think of. If somebody else was with her he would surely die.

"Hey Swig! Hey man!!!!" Kelly yelled out to where Swig was still moving around the dope.

"What!"

"Give this muthafucker 15 more of ours!"

"Why?" Swig asked.

"Just do it please!!"

"Man, that muthafucker done got all he's going to get from me, fuck that!" Swig now was delirious and wasn't to be trusted. Kelly-Boy jumped out of the truck, and walked to the back, and had a little talk with Swig.

Swig left Kelly standing there, looking stupid like he done lost his damn mind and got in the truck. He now sat there on the passenger side seat looking at Dirty like, "What's up!"

Dirty stared back at him like if he moved even an inch he would blow his little black ass out that passenger side window.

Once they were done Dirty headed home. It was now two in the morning he didn't have to work tomorrow, but his worries weren't over yet.

Dirty didn't use the front entrance of his house. Since he was trying to dodge his wife he had been using the side entrance of his basement. Dirty figured that Sophelia needed all the room he could give her; especially since he knew there wasn't enough room for them both.

CHAPTER 29 - SLEPT LATE

Dirty woke up and saw that Sophelia was gone. He walked up to the kitchen to get something to eat when breakfast was already prepared. He made a plate and, before going back downstairs, he got the newspaper from the front porch.

As he ate and drank a fresh cup of orange juice he flipped through the newspaper and found nothing about the murder, or the gun that killed J.J. Then he realized that it had happened too late last night to make it into this morning's paper. Dirty looked at the time; it was 11:45 a.m. He thought he would catch the 12:00 News on TV.

Dirty rolled a blunt after he was done feeding his face; today he was going to enjoy himself and just kick back. He had enough dope to start a drug war here in Charlotte, N.C. Then the News come on and said. "We have a breaking story here at 12:00 noon when we return." Dirty knew this was what he'd being waiting for.

Even all the dope and all the money couldn't add up to changing his mind about ever loving Sophelia the way he use too. She had crossed a line and he would have preferred for her to just keep that to herself. Something he couldn't figure out about why she would even just tell him that unless she wanted out of the marriage.

The news came back on with, "Late last night there was a home invasion that left a man dead and a woman alive, she couldn't identify any of the suspects, surely the young lady was afraid for her life. But in the process of searching the house the victim that was killed became a suspect in the murder of an officer that was shot and killed. During a search of the residence a gun that is believed to have been used in the killing of Officer

Jay Hookmore was found. The investigation is on-going and the Chief of Police had this to say: "We are all pleased that we were able to find the murder weapon, but our main concern was WHY Officer Hookmore was murdered."

Then Dirty said out loud "WHY IN THE FUCK does it matter? We got the murder weapon!"

The Chief went on to say, "The family is now relieved, but still sad about the tragedy of losing a family member as well as the young man that lost his life in this home invasion, Thank You!"

"Wait, could you please give use a little insight on the officer that lost his life?" the reporter asked.

"Officer Hookmore was a fine and outstanding police officer who patrolled these communities to make sure that it is safe for citizens to walk the streets of Charlotte, that's all I have to say for now!"

Dirty still wasn't satisfied with what he had just heard, he knew the Chief had left out key parts of the story, and he was sure the Chief knew more than what he was saying.

Dirty thought how his wife had let him down and now he had time to spread dope throughout the city of Charlotte. His main concern right now was Justine who appeared to still have a diva mentality. She had said this was far from being over. If this bitch even thought she could handle Dirty she had a surprise coming. Dirty's least worry was a woman.

Dirty heard a vehicle door close outside and he got up to check on who had just pull in the drive-way.

It was Sophelia and his son, who looked so much like his mother. Dirty watched the way his wife moved. How, with every step she had a twist in her hips. He could remember like yesterday when he had first laid eyes on her at a banquet, a Police Ball. He had spotted her talking to some of his colleagues. She'd been wearing these dress pants that fit her thighs to perfection and she had a low haircut revealing her Tom-Boyish style. She had looked as though she was determined to apply and bend the rules if she had too.

Carlos watched his family come up the stairs to the front door, when he went to greet his son. "Daddy, Daddy!!!!"

"What's up son? You miss your daddy! Huh?"

"Hmmmmm...mommy took me for pizza, and cake."

"Yeah? Mommy took time to do that for your son?"

"Yeah!"

Sophelia stood there while Dirty embraced his son, she had her arms crossed looking at her husband and trying to figure out something that now was bothering her. There was no doubt that she loved Carlos, but she thought how he had changed into someone she no longer knew.

"Come on! Today is my off day! What you want to do?"

"Let's you, me, and mommy go see a movie!" The son said looking at his parents.

That one hit Dirty in the gut because that's exactly what they use to do together. Sophelia looked up and she and Dirty now looked each other in the eyes.

Dirty said, "Yeah! We can do that! Ask mommy if she wants to come first!"

"Mommyyyyy... little Carlos dragged the name out while running to his mother and said again, "Please mommy!"

"Let's go," Sophelia replied softy as if she couldn't believe her husband would agree to translate something through their son.

CHAPTER 30 - JUSTINE

"Come in dad!" Justine said to her father with her eyes still swollen from crying hysterically from the evasion that she had survived.

Speedy embraced his daughter because she was his life and meant the world to him. Justine had never been the type to interfere in her father's business, and she knew not to talk to the police. She was trained coming up in her own family to never help the enemy.

Speedy had his main man, Murk, come along with him this time. He sat down with them and listened to Justine.

"Dad! I'm telling you this cop that Rat was telling us about came into our home and planted the gun here. I saw him face to face before he left the house and told him this was far from being over. This same fucking cop come in our old apartment before I even knew he was a cop dressed in regular clothes and smoked a blunt with me!" Justine told her father everything except that she had fucked him. Already she had been labeled as a piece of ass.

"What about the drugs?" Speedy asked. It seemed that's the only thing that he was concerned about.

"They took everything, and blowed a hole in Rat's head."

"I told you that Pat-Rat was too soft for this type of business. He wasn't supposed to never let them cops play him like that from the beginning. Look Honey, Hmmm...Murk is going to be putting some time in with you. Show him all the places around Charlotte; give him anything he needs to get my dope back!

"Murk! Justine! Justine! Murk!" Speedy said, disturbed and highly upset that anyone even thought he would take a loss like that.

Speedy walked to the car and got in the driver's seat of the vehicle while Murk grabbed his bags then Speedy drove off.

Justine showed Murk where he was sleeping and left his room while he got situated.

Justine went to the internet and strolled public safety with the Police Department trying to find out who was Carlos.

Finally, after Murk was done placing his things, he came in the living room and had a seat. "Murk," is 6' 1" and weighed about 215 pounds: a real solid dude who dressed conservatively. He had a nice, trim goatee wave leaning to the side. He looked like a business man, but was a straight killer, who done the job extremely well. Murk had a charming smile and Justine had certainly noticed.

Murk lived in a world thinking life had no boundaries, no morals or sensitivity to any life that had to be killed. His mother was a very hard worker who worked for every dollar that was made to pay the bills. She worked as a registered nurse on the night shift to support her family. Murk was the only kid, at least that's what he was told. And his Pop who hustled and depended on every dollar he schemed for.

On this particular day everyone caught on to the games and witnessed how Murk's father would win every night and take away their winnings. The word got around how Murk's father had been hustling them. Even the niggas that didn't have anything to do with this particular game, but had lost to him before, paid Murk's father a surprise visit. When Murk's father answered the door, he was looking into a barrel of a pump shotgun. The gun walked him back into the house with the barrel pressed against his nose. Murk, at the age of 9, got under the kitchen table and witnessed his father get his head blown completely off. Then his mother, who had nothing to do with it, had a hole blowed in her chest.

Justine sat crying on the computer when Murk said. "Hmmm, excuse me for asking, but at the same time no disrespect, why cry when it's impossible to bring back the lost. Listen to this; I learned it from a friend: The calls of death are always for the best, for we are solving problems there as well as here, and one is sure to find himself where he can solve his problems best. It is selfishness that makes one wish to call again to earth's departed souls. So let that be an inspiration to you so you are able to celebrate his home coming; a destiny that is uncertain and unknown.

For a minute Justine couldn't relate to what he just said, she thought how Murk spoke with authority assuring her that death is no enemy of man, when his work of life is done.

Justine couldn't find anything on the computer far as the information she needed.

"How come I never met you before Murk?" Justine questioned the good looking man who was older than her but who had just confided in her.

"Let's just say I stay out of the spot light, something I never thought about getting accustomed to."

"That's not the answer I was looking for!" Justine said trying to disguise her swollen eyes and not feeling sexy at all.

"Okay okay, pardon me! Where have you been during the time of my life when I needed that special someone I could look in the eyes, like I'm looking at you now, come here and give me a hug." Murk just wanted to comfort Justine and not so much seduce her because he had come here to do a job and he meant to do it; the dope is what Speedy was concerned about.

CHAPTER 31 - "HOT SPOT"

"Yo! That's the way you going to play a nigga Kelly-Boy? After all the shit we been through; me watching your back, and this is the appreciation I get?"

"Look here man! I'll give you one of them things!"

"One?! I should be able to get what's left! You fucking trying to play me Kelly!" Swig said.

"Calm down; it's not that serious. If it makes you happy Swig, I'll give you three more. Damn you act like you forgetting the police taking care of our pending charges we're on bond with."

"You ain't thinking; especially with all the shit I've done for you!"

"You right, fuck boy!"

"Fuck Boy!"

"Yeah that's what you calling me in this situation"

"This ain't what you want Kelly-Boy! Just let me get the other three and I'm out," Swig said looking crazy, and extremely sure of himself.

"That's a small thing to a giant partner! Hey Wet, come here. Look in my truck and get two more of them things for me please!"

"Three!" Swig yelled out.

"Yeah! Give him three. There you go partner. Oh yeah give your car keys to Wet, yeah that's right; since you wanted that third one."

"Shit, that third one going to buy me something bigger than what you got partner!" Swig hid the four kilos in the brushes, and waited for his girl to show up with his ride.

Kelly-Boy and Wet watched him pull off and Kelly yelled out, "Don't spend it all in one place. You know what man? You remember them charges against us?"

"Yeah!" Wet replied.

"I took care of them charges for us, and this is the thanks I get, because that stupid muthafucker can't think! What good is that dope if you gotta do 30 years in prison?"

"He'll be back! His girlfriend tricks Swig out of his money every time."

"Shit no!!!! He come back around here, Wet, his ass up. Shit, we Crips anyway, didn't that nigga use to be a blood?" Kelly asked.

Wet tried to figure out where Kelly was going with this, because Wet and Swig come up in the hood together, they'd always respected each other. "Let that nigga go on about his business; the nigga love you Kelly-Boy! To be honest, we talked and I can't see Swig coming back fucking with you, not to hurt you."

"Either you down with me or you are against me. Fuck them feelings; leave that shit to them hoes. Money don't have feelings. That cheese (Money) helps you build a foundation to keep the prey as well as the enemy away."

"This all I'm saying Kelly: You fell out with a friend of mine, and I didn't have no beef with Swig, and you expect for me to fill his shoes, and drive his car that you gave him that everybody knows is his -"

"Wait, wait!" Kelly said.

"No listen! Let me finish - then kill him for y'all greed, if that's all you can use me for then I'm not welcomed here. We were a team; if anything, give me the same respect you gave to Swig before and let me buy my own shit. Regardless, whether you know this or not, I'm a loyal brother."

"Hey! You right! I see now we are gonna be a helluva team, not that I didn't know. But you refused to let money come between us when that's all I'm use to dealing with. Them be the same ones to come back and be ready to hit me in the head. But you going to fuck around and get me killed, shit I know that you mean good."

Kelly-Boy knew then, what he didn't know before - that Wet is real! Kelly-Boy never took the time to see who Wet was as a person.

"Wet, you gave me a world of awakening. Sometimes you get caught up in the drug game, and I barely have enough time for myself. You know for real I was ready to kill him, luckily whatever you seen in me as a person it was easy for you to embrace.

"It's just I come up with six brothers, and two were killed. That left me with some experiences about making decisions on my own, and my brothers weren't fortunate enough to do that for themselves."

"Hold up partner! You in the wrong game!" Kelly replied, smiling ear to ear."

"See! There you go again."

"Alright, alright! Let's get this money.

LEAVING HOME

Dirty left Sophelia in the bed because, after a whole day of family activities yesterday, she needed to rest. Dirty thought how it was funny how a kid, who was loved so dearly, had brought them back together when he thought it was impossible.

Dirty had several voice messages from last night; he had been unable to get to the phone because his dick was stuck in Sophelia ass. Freak ass bitch, he thought, if he would've been the first to sodomize his own wife he wouldn't have thought less of her, but just the thought of another man sexing his wife in the ass was enough for him to want to drop her like a bad habit.

Dirty parked and went inside the police precinct, grabbing a hot cup of coffee as usual, but before he could sit down at his desk the Chief waved for Dirty to come into his office. He walked in the office and looked to see if anyone was watching.

"Close the door, and have a seat," the Chief said fumbling through something.

Dirty sat quietly while the Chief looked through some papers, and then his phone rang. For a moment Dirty's heart pumped faster than it had every done. With his mind racing, wondering what the fuck could the Chief possibly want? Dirty finally saw the papers the Chief had in his hand when he turned to retrieve something for the caller on the phone. It was an affidavit form.

"You see what I'm holding? Wait, not this one, but this here," the Chief said.

"Yeah, it's a report," Dirty replied.

"Okay son! Help me understand this whole ordeal please! Maybe something went wrong, how does a street drug dealer come in here asking for help? Luckily he was referred to me and not the Feds because we didn't have the slightest idea what officer the drug dealer were talking about. But we knew the area; when the young man said Carlos, so I signed J.J. to the case to see if these allegations were true. Of course he lied for you, and said nothing! But the guy claimed you were trying to extort him! Now he's come up dead son! With the gun that was used to kill J.J.! Something ain't adding up right. Me personally, I think you need to cover your tracks a little better then you are doing. I'm going to say this: there are people out there who know people."

Dirty sat there and listened to the Chief knowing that he wasn't about to tell on himself, especially when both men were dead. If he wanted to understand then Dirty thought he should've been a part of the problem rolling with him instead of against him looking for information to throw away the key on a nigga for life.

"Son, I find it hard to believe that you don't know more than what you're telling me. Just keep J.J.'s family, and him, in your prayers," the Chief said looking puzzled.

Dirty left out and thought the only place he was going to keep J.J. is in that grave where he wouldn't have to worry about a dead man saying shit.

Dirty sat at the desk momentary, and thought about what was next. He had 52 kilos - more than enough - but the question was how could he push it without running into the Feds? He looked around the room; the chemistry was different. He didn't want to be here anymore than he had to be. Eyes watched him and he knew something wasn't right. Whatever they knew couldn't be any more than what was on the police report.

Grabbing his coffee Dirty rushed for the door and left. Once inside his cruiser he grabbed his cell phone to call Sophelia; for what, he really didn't know when she picked up.

"Good morning Honey!" She said, excited for some reason.

"You mean good afternoon!"

"It's only em....oh God! Where's my baby at?"

"Calm down! His grandparents came and got him, like he made them complete or something, they refuse to let a day go by without him."

"Baby I miss you, where you at right now?" Sophelia asked in her sexy voice, vulnerable and in need.

"Baby? What happen to Carlos?" Dirty asked.

"It's only Carlos when you act crazy, but right now I need you here with me," she answered.

"Well I hate to spoil the moment, because I'm at work. I'm sitting in my car at the police precinct and thought I should call my wife; something that I miss doing. After yesterday, I never knew what tomorrow would bring, but what it brought was more than what I had anticipated. When I thought it was hard for me to ever love again how I once loved you,' he said waiting on a response as it got quiet for a seconds.

"I really did mess up, only you really know how much I love you. I'm asking you to forgive me if you can find it in your heart?" she replied waiting to hear what Carlos had to say.

"You know this isn't like a light switch that you can turn on and off," said Carlos.

"I know Honey! Lord knows I know!" Sophelia cried.

"But what you done didn't make it right for me to do it either, even though it's a lot more severe when it's a woman, and she's your wife. Let's work on it one day at a time".

"I respect that; a chance is what I'm asking for anyway, without it we would have nothing."

"Later!" Said Carlos.

"Wait! At least tell me you love me!

"You didn't give me a chance too."

"What if we didn't have any chance?"

"I love you!" Dirty said as he hung up the phone.

CHAPTER 33 - JUSTINE, MURK

Murk was patiently waiting for Justine to get off work. He sat in silence cleaning his 45 magnum with a rag and drinking a glass of liquor. Breaking the pistol all the way down, he had taken off everything that would come off.

Murk was a very dedicated dude, especially to his professional ability, but right now he only had 45 minutes before Justine was due home.

He jumped in the shower trying to bring down the feeling from the alcohol. Once he was finished Murk dried off and sat back on the same couch where he was before. But this time butt azz-naked still sipping his alcohol.

There were sounds of keys at the door, and Justine walked through the door. Stunned, but amazed she was looking at the sexy view of a man she would've never thought would be as open and expressive as he was. Justine thought how he was too real to be true; sitting there on her furniture ass naked, and not to expecting anything to happen.

Justine dropped her keys and fell to both knees and knew the package deal was for her. Justine grabbed the dick, and licked around the head then in one complete deep throat when Murk said, "Go take a quick wash up". He helped her up, letting her use his forearm for support as he stood with her. Then gripping her ass with a nice firm grip before she walked away dragging her hands across his chest.

As Justine was walking away, twisting her ass as she pulled down her dress, Murk was checking out the thong that disappeared between her thick ass-cheeks. She never looked back to see his facial expression.

Murk was filled with the eagerness of pleasure before handling business. He felt vulnerable because the alcohol made him feel like she was all he had in this world. Murk didn't give a fuck about Justine being Speedy's daughter, and at the same time he knew this was a violation of the rules.

As Murk sipped his drink, and hearing the shower running in the bath room, he got up and went to the guest bedroom. When he returned he was fully dressed. He looked at Justine as she stood butt naked like she needed to be touched, and loved, but she had a disappointed look on her face as if she couldn't believe how quickly he had changed his mind. "I'm sorry, maybe later," he said as he held her face in both hands looking into her eyes with a lot of love and concern.

"Why can't we do it? Don't you find me attractive?" she asked while looking in his eyes. Justine wanted to trade out on some of that dick she had in her mouth earlier.

"That's a crazy question sweetie; you are more beautiful now that I see you like this. I never rush the moment when I want it to last a life time."

Justine really thought that the reason he didn't want to do it was because there was something wrong with her. Murk embraced her and, while doing so, he caressed her ass and breathed along side of her neck where her hot spot was located.

* * *

PENTHOUSE

"Oh God! I'ma be in trouble!" Regina said as she pulled the glass dick from her mouth. Monica, and CeCe had left, as usual, to go shopping; something they enjoyed doing with their money.

"Why are you worrying about them Bitches for? Shit....fuck them!" Said Craig, the crack-head who lived next-door to her husband. He had once been Regina's downfall because listening to him the first time is why she got kicked out. This was the same nigga.

"Look! You got to go! And I mean quick, because they are on their way back now!" Regina said, so paranoid and wanting Craig to get his ass out.

"Girl you just paranoid; that dope good, ain't it?"

"Get out! Here take this shit with you please!" She said.

"You sure?" Craig asked, holding it in his palm and reviewing what she might be missing.

Finally Regina closed the door behind him and thought how she never wanted to see him again. Craig's crack-headed ass was the reason she lost her husband. Her biggest worry was him showing back up on her steps uninvited, looking for a couple of dollars from her to support his habit. Giving him money was something she should've never started doing.

Regina went to her room and jumped in the cold shower. She shivered as the cold water brought her down from the high. She started crying and knew she needed help, and she never wanted to get high again.

She got out of the shower and tried to pretend that this never happened, knowing she was only trying to fool herself. She put her makeup on and went into the kitchen to pour herself a drink.

Dirty was all she could think about. If he had the slightest idea she was back to smoking, she would be out of a place to live and back on the streets where he'd found her.

After a minute she heard somebody at the door and her heart just about dropped out of her chest hoping it wasn't Craig wanting money. Then the door opened revealing Monica and CeCe laughing like they'd had an enjoyable time shopping. She wished she had gone with them.

"Hey Girl! What's wrong? You look a hot mess! Are you okay?" CeCe asked being concerned and caring for her girl, whom she had developed a close relationship with.

"Yeah! Why would you say that?" Regina replied, trying to straighten her face because the high had her paranoid.

"Are you high Bitch!?" Monica asked, being up front and direct.

Regina tried to defend herself with an attitude not confessing to something that would get her kicked out of the penthouse because this was the best thing going for her. She knew her getting high would jeopardize the other women's careers.

"Look Regina! Look at me girl! If you've done something and regret doing it, tell us so we can make preparations to help you with your addiction. You lying is not going to help none at all, especially when we on your side." CeCe said.

By this time they didn't have to say another word when Regina dropped in tears.

"Man! I knew this bitch was lying, girl!" Monica said like she thought Regina was out of her damn mind.

CHAPTER 34 - PLENTY OF WORK

Dirty couldn't stop thinking about Justine. There should've been two dead at the murder scene. Dirty thought how he could never stop thinking about how she looked him in the eyes and said something that was going to always keep him on alert.

Then Dirty had a plan; he wanted Justine dead for real. He decided to call Kelly-Boy and see what's up with him.

The phone rang continuously as Dirty sat there waiting patiently when Kelly-Boy said "Yeah! What's up?"

"Can I meet you somewhere?" Dirty asked.

"Who is this?"

"Dirty!"

"Shit! The way you handled me? Hell no! For what?"

"Look! I'm not trying to put my business out like that!" Dirty said frustrated.

"I wanna know what you driving?"

"I'm driving the cruiser."

"The police car?"

"Yeah, man damn! Are you that stupid?!" said Dirty.

"That's what you want me to be; yeah I'm stupid! What the fuck do you want, you dirty muthafucker?"

"I'm trying to do some business, and give you some of them things back."

"I'll meet you at the gas station on Cinderella St, and Sugar Creek Rd." said Kelly-Boy.

"When?"

"I'm already here in the store." Click.

Dirty thought it would be just as easy to just shoot Kelly-Boy in the head and deal with Justine himself.

Dirty pulled in on Cinderella and Sugar Rd. at the store where he spotted Kelly's car sitting higher than the shield over the gas pump. Dirty thought how stupid this nigga really was just looking out the window and drinking an energy drink. He pulled in beside Kelly-Boy's car, not wanting to look obvious and suspicious about how they were meeting.

Walking out the store Kelly-Boy jumped in his car and sat up high so he could see every movement that Dirty might make.

"You see them folks in the store, them my people they watching my back," said Kelly-Boy.

"Listen here you stupid muthafucker! If I wanted to do something to you they couldn't stop me," Dirty said, kinda mad that Kelly-Boy would play with his intelligence when it was business he was trying to conduct with this ignorant ass nigga.

"What! What is it man...? You calling me all these names like I won't bust a grape!" exclaimed Kelly-Boy.

"I got 10 kilos for Justine's life?" said Dirty.

"Where they at? Shit, you should've told me that out the gate!"

"Take this number here, and call me when it's handled. I don't give a fuck when you do it, as long as it's done before tomorrow."

"Damn! That's not enough time! Why you want all these folks dead?"asked Kelly-Boy.

"Don't worry about that, can you handle the job?"

"Yeah! But don't try to take my life afterwards, you dirty azz cop!"

"Bye."

"Wait! Wait, where the bitch living at now?"

"The same house." Dirty said driving off.

Dirty drove down Sugar Creek Road on Timmbrook Street where he once arrested the jay-walker. Dirty approached the cul-de-sac. Then like before the dealer came out and sat on the porch Dirty pointed for him to come here. Dude got up brushing off his butt and walked to the police car and said. "How can I help you, officer?"

"You want the honest to God truth?" Dirty replied, trying to put on a friendly face so he was able to make dude feel comfortable with his presence.

"Please! You wanna save me some time from this embarrassment with me just looking foolish standing out here talking to a Cop?"

"Take my business card! Can you handle five kilo's?" Dirty asked, trying to look through his eyes and out the back of his head.

The dude smirked with the card inside his hands, and walked away looking at Dirty.

Dirty said, "It's more when you done with that!"

Pulling off looking in his review mirror, Dirty knew he had to start somewhere instead of letting the dope set around the crib.

Turning on Power 97.9 and listening to that Little Wayne... "I'm on fire man.... I'm on fire man..."

Then the Dispatcher alerted.

(911 DISPATCH)

"We have a man that was shot off Plaza Road on Pecan Avenue in front of the Dairy Ice Cream Shop; possibility a life threatening situation."

Dirty was two minutes away. He ran the stop lights and when he arrived, there laid a man that appeared to be shot in head.

Quickly Dirty got out and ran to the young man that probably wasn't no more than 20 years old; a black male. Dirty felt for a pulse, but the young man was dead. Blood poured from the temple.

It wasn't a pretty sight to see. The ambulance arrived along with the fire truck. Dirty looked over his shoulder and saw a man standing there at the side door entrance of the ice cream place holding his gun, and Dirty yelled, "Drop your weapon, NOW!!" as he drew his gun.

The man's wife grabbed the gun from her husband and put it on ground, when two other cars approached the cops jumped out and bum rushed him, and threw the man to the ground. Searching the man and dragging him to his feet they placed him in the back seat of the police car.

Dirty walk over to the lady and said, "Who is the man that we arrested?"

"That's my husband!" the lady cried obviously close to hysteria.

"What happened?"

"That man was going to rob us!" The lady screamed holding the side of her face like she was hysterical.

"So, is this the gun the robber had?" Dirty ask pointing at the gun he retrieved from her husband.

"No!"

"Where is his gun? Calm down Mrs., where is his gun?" Dirty kept asking.

"Wait here!" Dirty followed her, being cautious with her movement.

When the lady returned, she handed Dirty a note that appeared to come from the robbery.

Dirty read it, it said: "This is a robbery give me some of the money."

That was it, as Dirty turned the piece of paper over a few times looking for something that was supposed to been life-threatening. He then walked over to the homicide Detective to get a better understanding of why this man had to die over a note, a piece of paper that wasn't asking for all the money just "some of the money".

The police congregated together, some laughed; they couldn't believe that this tragedy happened over a damn note.

Dirty walked back to his car. The man was sitting in the back seat of another vehicle now. Dirty looked at the man who was looking at him like he couldn't stand a nigga. Dirty thought he was about to get everything he asked for, he was sure a mandatory life sentence was in this man's near future.

Dirty wasn't going to entertain his manipulation of bad judgment in character because dude probable didn't like Blacks. Dirty didn't want the pleasure of taking this idiot Downtown. Then again Dirty thought how they had some of the same similarities when Dirty cared nothing about killing a nigga.

CHAPTER 35 - DAIRY QUEEN

Dirty pulled out of the parking lot of the Dairy Queen and decided to ride by the penthouse. Dirty Knew he was close to fucking Regina and that he needed to retreat and regain control of himself until Justine was dead.

In the parking lot of the penthouse, Dirty noticed a few cars parked. He was puzzled about Justine, and the way she looked him in the eyes. She acted as if she was in control of herself; but there was something else there too that he couldn't get a total hold on.

Dirty sat there in his cruiser for almost 45 minutes when he realized he didn't want to scare away the customers. One thing was for sure, them ho's were doing some fucking. So Dirty pulled out of the parking lot. It was five more hours before he was off.

* * *

Kelly-Boy wanted so bad to handle this for Dirty, but he knew his chance with "Wet" would be slim-to-none. Kelly couldn't suck his pride in to call Swig, but as much as he liked Wet, he called Swig.

The phone rang about six times when Kelly hung up and thought how this nigga was in his feelings. Kelly opened the door of his bedroom where Red, his girl, laid butt ass naked; just the way Kelly liked it. His phone rang; it was Swig returning his phone call.

"Yeah, this Swig."

"Hey, dawg! What's up?"

"You tell me, shit you called me," said Swig.

"Hey man that's not for us! You feel me?"

"What's up Kelly?"

"Damn! You alright?" Kelly held one hand in the air like he was trying to get some understanding.

"Yeah! It's my girl getting on my damn nerve, that's all."

"Hey, Dawg!" What I tell you about them women?" Said Kelly.

"Yeah, I know what you said about them hoes. I bet yours is butt ass naked on the bed?"

"Watch your mouth! But damn sure is, but hey listen to this."

Kelly went on to explain to Swig about the set-up with ole girl, but Kelly didn't really want any involvement with killing the bitch. But money and dope were in the air just waiting for someone to claim it.

Kelly knew Swig didn't have any remorse for nobody besides his mother and all he needed was a minute to think about it. He couldn't stop thinking about how that dirty ass cop done took everything he had. And Kelly wanted it back.

Kelly-Boy hung up with Swig then went back in the bedroom with sexy, beautiful, "Red," who Kelly actually paid for every second and minute of the day to have her as his bitch. She spent most of her time in the mall when she wasn't in the house walking around butt naked.

Kelly pulled off his clothes and Red said, "Did you take a shower?," she asked with her head turned slightly toward him, watching him as he pulled off his clothes

"Yeah Baby! You mean the bath you going to give me with your tongue!"

"What do you mean by that? Sucking your nasty ass dick? Shit! I don't think so."

"Don't I suck your pussy?"

"So! You're supposed to take care of your Goddess!"

"And you're supposed to take care of your King."

"Yeah, but you never made me suck your dick!"

"Come here! There you go put it in your mouth."

Red acted if she was a stranger to the fact while she held Kelly's dick looking around the head part, as if she wasn't too sure it was safe to do. So Kelly grabbed her head and forced his dick to her lips and once she had it in her mouth she turned pro with the sloppy sucking as Red marinated his nut at the same time.

Kelly looked at Red's shoulders and neck as she ate the dick in rotation and he reached and pressed up and down her back, rubbing her soft skin. Her back arched as he watched between the crack of her ass-cheeks as her firm ass would jump at times. Her long hair lay on the side of her neck, the diamonds that Kelly-Boy had brought her sparkling on her fingers. He thought from now on this is where he wanted his dick to be; down her throat. Besides, Kelly liked it better, being wet in her mouth with no rubber, than in her pussy with the rubber that she always made him wear.

She lay on her stomach still sucking his dick while he now ate out of her ass like she liked, giving her the feeling she enjoyed. Kelly opened both ass-cheeks while he put his tongue in her ass, as Red moaned. All you could hear was smacking sound from both ends, when Kelly tried taking the dick out her mouth, because she knew now that Kelly wanted to fuck.

"Where is your rubber? You know I'm not on nothing"

"Hey, look here, I told you last week to get a shot. Didn't I give you the money for it?" He said in a low voice, being sexy while being in the mood.

"I forgot baby!" she cried, begging for another chance.

"Turn around."

"But Kelly!"

"Turn your ass this way, go ahead now, I'm not gonna nut inside of you, I promise!"

"I don't want to catch nothing!"

"What!? You saying I got something?"

"No I'm not...."

"Turn your ass around then Baby, come on, there you go." Red now was in the doggy-style position as Kelly played with the head in her bushy pink pussy. In the eight months that they had been together, this was their first time having unprotected sex.

Kelly-Boy spread her ass-cheeks and made faces behind her like he couldn't believe he had finally touched base inside of Red.

After a few minutes, he busted off inside of her. That nutt got Kelly feeling cocky and ensured her if she get pregnant he would pay for it.

CHAPTER 36 - UNEXPECTED PHONE CALL

After getting off work and driving home Dirty walked in the front door of his house. To his left Sophelia was on the computer. Dirty walked over and kissed his wife passionately.

"How was your day?" She asked, looking at her husband in a seductive way.

"It was long and frustrating; a young man got killed over a note to rob a Dairy Queen ice cream parlor.

"You got to be kidding me!" She replied wondering what the world was coming to.

"I'ma take a shower, how's business?"

"Great!" They just barely had enough time for themselves.

Dirty walked off seeing the smirk that Sophelia had on her face.

Once Dirty was downstairs he opened his vault and grabbed a bag that was left and rolled five blunts up. His cell phone started ringing. He wanted to push void because at the moment he felt so relaxed and didn't want to be bothered.

"Hello! This is Carlos, how can I help you?"

"This is Kingston!"

"I'm sorry but I think that you have the wrong number! You said Kingston? Hmmm... I'm trying to figure out where I heard that name before?"

"You gave me your business card, remember, Carlos? Or do you do that to all the killers you meet?"

"That's not the name you gave me the other day, right?"

For a minute Carlos thought how the fuck he knew his name. Then that explained how he knew his name.

"Shit! Let's be realistic, you're the Po, Po you expect for a nigga to tell on him damn self! Huh?"

"Nah! But if I'm expecting to do business at least I expect you to keep it real!"

"How the fuck you know about the spot? First, tell me that shit." Kingston said, waiting on a answer.

"You damn self-serving nigga! Dope like that is hard to find, you feel me?" said Dirty.

"Okay Cop! Let's get money, other than that we don't have shit in common, do I make myself clear Carlos?"

"Tell me what you can move?"

"Whatever, it doesn't matter; I can move somebody's house and turn each brick into a home."

"You talk a good game! Where can we meet?"

"I like that, something tell me you're about business; lets meet where you always park in front of a nigga's crib," Kingston said being funny.

"When?"

"I'm here!"

"Yeah, I'm on my way".

Dirty knew the law took chances as easy as the niggas running flagging down cars on the blocks trying to make a sale. But Dirty felt good about this one.

He quickly jumped in the shower, trying to meditate as the hot water splashed on his body. Closing his eyes Dirty almost forgot where he was. He felt a pair of hands wrapping around his stomach. Sophelia had joined him and pressed her face against his neck realizing how much she loved Carlos more than ever.

Sophelia's hair was loose and hanging below her shoulders on both sides as she massaged his dick from where she stood. Dirty turned with his dick extended hitting Sophelia's stomach, he tongue kissed his wife and they drug their tongues across each other, as water splashed and nursed their bodies.

Dirty grabbed the bar of soap and caressed it, making his hands soapy, and grabbed between her ass-cheeks and he penetrated a finger into her rectum. He turned her kind of hard, making her spread her hands across the shower wall and entered her ass. Dirty now had penetrated her ass and gripped the top of her forehead with the inner part of his biceps.

"Baby...ahhh...ahhh...ahhh...ahh...., I love you honey. Yeah..." as Dirty pounded her ass-cheeks he couldn't figure it out why she loved the dick so much in her ass. He felt her nipples with the other free hand and they were rock hard. He kissed all over her neck in her hot spot, but right now what was even hotter was her ass. His body felt numb, she would tighten up her ass-cheeks where Dirty could no longer take it and busted off inside of her waste bucket. She then turned around putting her arms under his and pressed her face on Dirty chest as if there was no other place she would rather be in the world. Dirty felt the embrace and smelled the top of her head. He could remember the first time he ever smelled her scent.

Finally, after they were done, he dried his wife off and walked her to the bedroom as they both got dressed. Dirty went downstairs and grabbed seven kilos of cocaine and placed them in the back of his wife's S.U.V. and left.

Coming down Sugar Creek only a few blocks away, Dirty thought how he was playing his hands, and not wanting continue to sit on all the dope he had in his house. Dirty pulled in on Timmerbrook, and drove down in the cul-de-sac and pulled along the circle checking out the set then drove back up the street until he could feel comfortable with himself. Then went back and parked where he usually sat watching Kingston's spot.

Dirty cut off his engine and looked in all the directions he possibly could when all of a sudden Kingston jumped in his little hooptie, then backed out where he now was beside Dirty's vehicle rolling down his window.

"Follow me!" Kingston said.

Dirty pulled off following Kingston and didn't have the slightest idea where dude was taking him. They got to the end of the street where a storage room was located. Patiently waiting for the gate to come open, Kingston pulled around to where they were parked in a blind side. Kingston then got out where he and Dirty was face to face. "Before I accept anything from you, are you the police," Kingston asked.

"Yeah, I'm an off-duty cop; but what difference does that make? If I wanted to bust your ass, I could've done that a while ago."

"What you got for me?"

"For right now just a little something."

Dirty open the back of the S.U.V. for the seven kilos. Kingston walked over and noticed the seal on the packages that looked so familiar.

"So this is it?" Kingston asked.

"Nah! There's more where that came from, after you're done with them."

"You know it's been real dry around here. To be honest, the price can go up."

"Look, I don't care, just give me 21g's for each one, the sooner you finish, I'll get back at you.

Kingston grabbed the kilos and put them in the storage room. Dirty thought how that was a good place to store his dope, but Dirty knew the closer his dope was to him the better.

The first thing Dirty was going to do was look Kingston up on his computer, and see who he was dealing with. But there was no question he was a street nigga.

CHAPTER 37 - TRAP HOUSE

"What is he paying for the bitch? Whatever it is I know this cop is dirty as hell," Swig said hungry and ready to get paid.

"It's about dark now; I'm ready to do this!" Kelly-Boy replied.

"You think that bitch still stay there by herself?"

"Shit, that's what the Cop told me."

"He knocking people off with their own dope, then killing them! Shit, we need to be careful with this muthafucker he might get us!" Swig said looking concerned about what he'd got himself into.

"I'm concerned about the dope he took from us partner. Shit I want more," Kelly-Boy said.

"So what's up with "Wet" is he going too?" Swig asked, wondering why they didn't pick him up.

"Nah! I can't fuck with him on that level partner, he's nothing like us! You heard?"

"Shit...! I have known "Wet" all my life! That's what he does; how do you think he'd got that name?"

"Look here dawg! It's just me, and you. We got to be careful this time; it's a different game plan now. When it gets real dark where no one will be able to see us, we'll creep up around the house. Shit, we might be able to burn her ass up without going in the house," Kelly said.

"How much is in it for us to kill this bitch? I want to know before I even attempt this. Something ain't right with this police. Let's tax his ass the same way he taxed us for taking care of our charges." Swig said.

"We are going to get back what he took from us from the beginning."

"Yeah, every last one of them."

Time was pushing along and Kelly agreed to give back Swig's car and told him he should've never taken it from him in the first place, then they bull-shitted for awhile until they felt the urge to make a move.

It was like 12:30 at night when Kelly-Boy and Swig jumped into the little four door hooptie. As Kelly drove a thought occurred to him and he said, "Swig you right! This bitch knows something or got something on this cop. I believe he's putting a hit on this bitch with their own dope! And what is surprising is she's still living after all the dope she got robbed of. Look here man, let's handle this, then I'll tell this pig don't call us no more. This shit going to be on the News like never before partner, you hear me!?"

"What about the last one, was it on the News?" Swig asked.

"I don't know! I heard it from someone else in the streets."

Kelly and Swig arrived and they drove past the house and saw the little car that was backed up in the driveway. Just about 100 yards down the street they got out and walked back up the street slowly, watching the few houses with the lights off.

Swig stepped on some broken glass and it crunched loudly in the silence of the night.

* * *

INSIDE THE HOUSE

Murk got up quickly and went in Justine's bedroom and whispered for her to stay still and lay on the floor. He told her that they had some visitors outside.

Murk grabbed his .45 magnum and crawled on his hands and knees through the house, staying well below and away from the windows. He could still hear footsteps beside the house. Then he saw a shadow walking past the window.

Boom, boom, boom! Murk fired three times and heard somebody holler. He knew he had hit whoever it was outside the window and he went outside and looked around the corner. There on the ground was a man, still alive and trying to crawl away when Murk caught up.

"You hurt huh? What the fuck you doing creeping around people's windows?" Murk asked.

"I'm sorry man! We had the wrong house," he replied breathing real hard after being shot in his shoulder, drained and couldn't run because of the pain.

"C'mon let me help you to the hospital, is this your gun?"

"Yeah!"

"I'll put it up in the crib until we get back! Just lay there I'll be back!"

"Okay, I appreciated it man." He said grunting with pain holding his shoulder.

Murk went back inside the house and looked through the living room window and saw dude still laying there holding his shoulder.

"Look here Justine!" Murk said.

"What! Who is it?"

"Right there on the ground. Does the nigga look familiar?"

"I can't see, wait a minute, yeah! That's one of the dudes that killed Pat-Rat! What the fuck does he want?" Justine said shaking a little.

"What the fuck you think! Probably more drugs or you! Where are your car keys?"

"What are you about to do Murk?"

"Just give me the keys."

Murk went back outside and helped up dude to his feet and gave him a towel to wrap around his shoulders, and he tilted a bit getting in the car. Luckily the sound didn't carry through the night since Murk had fired from inside the house.

"What are y'all looking for? Why did your partner take off and leave you? He ain't shit!"

"Yeah fuck that nigga!" He said, barely able to say what he wanted because he was hurting and losing a lot of blood.

"Help me understand something." Said Murk.

"Yeah, what?"

"You niggas killed her boyfriend on a robbery! Now why would the fuck you niggas come back? Don't lie to me, you see this .45 magnum? Yeah this is the same gun that just put a hole in your ass, now the second one is going to kill you. Now think before you answer the question when I'm giving you the benefit of the doubt, one lie, just one, and I'll kill you quick!"

"Oh God! I'm sorry man," as he begged crying and realizing there was nothing he could do to defend himself if he wanted too.

"I'm waiting! Shit it won't be long before you bleed to death!"

"Yeah, I know! I need to go to the hospital bad; I'm hurting."

"The sooner you talk, the sooner I can take you."

"Me and my so-call partner done this for a cop!"

"Yeah! Go ahead I'm listening," said Murk.

"He said if we kill the girl, that we could get the dope back for what he took from us."

"Why did the cop do it? And where does this cop live so I can get this dope back?"

"I don't know; I swear

"Okay forget that, I can't take you to the hospital I'll have to let your boy take you, can you call him?"

"My phone is in the car," he said with pain raging through his body.

Murk convinced dude to let him know where he lived. They drove to Kelly-Boy's trap house where he and Wet were on the front porch.

Murk stopped at the end of the driveway and got a good look at the two.

"Tell your boys to get you to the hospital soon man, so you won't bleed to death." Murk said, showing some concern for a nigga.

"Shit! It might be a little late for that!" Swig said opening the passenger side door trying to get himself out.

Murk thought how these young niggas didn't know shit besides pointing a gun at a muthafucker. Once he was out Murk rolled down the window and said, "Yo Dude!"

Swig turned holding his shoulder in great pain as Kelly-Boy and Wet rushed in the direction to help Swig when they heard two loud sounds. Murk pump two holes in Swig's chest as Kelly and Wet stopped in their tracks then ran in the opposite direction.

CHAPTER 38 - TRAP HOUSE

"Damn! What the FUCK! Look here, Wet. The police will be here in a minute. What did you do with the drugs?" Kelly said, shook like muthafucker.

"Don't worry I hid them outside in the backyard. What the fuck are we going to tell the Cops?" Wet asked.

"We ain't telling them shit! We were in the house when it happened, then we ran outside and the car was gone."

Kelly-Boy and Wet stood over their lost friend as blood came from his mouth and nose. The police showed up, looking around the yard for a weapon. Swig was pronounced dead on the scene and Swig laid there in the driveway with a white sheet covering him for almost two hours before they removed his body.

Kelly-Boy and Wet had to go downtown to give a statement. They tried to explain that they knew nothing, but the Police thought that wasn't good enough.

Kelly sat in the back seat as he tried to figure out his next move. Should he tell Dirty about the accident or just let it ride? Kelly wasn't worrying about Wet talking because he really didn't know shit. But what kept beating Kelly-Boy's mind was how in the hell Swig got whoever that was to bring him home and then blow a hole in his ass. And what did Swig tell dude? Kelly knew he had to move his spot because dude left a message and it was clear that he meant business.

Finally pulling in at the police station, Kelly-Boy went inside with the Homicide Detective and Wet went elsewhere; splitting them up to see if their stories matched.

"Okay son, can I get you anything, what about a cigarette?"

"I got Newport! What's up po, po? I'm telling you I don't know shit! Everything I told you at the house is exactly what I'll tell you again. Am I under arrest? If not y'all need to let me go man," Kelly said with his eyes wide open like he was scared for no reason at all.

"Son, just relax. Nobody is blaming you for the murder; we just need the same statement so that we will have it on file and you will be free to go, now let's get this over with. Where were you around 12:00 a.m?"

"Man!! Didn't you ask me that a while ago? Don't even try it; you trying to twist my story now."

"Please sir! Just answer the damn questions!" The police said trying to be intimidating.

"That's the way you talk to people you are questioning?"

"If I have to tell you again Sir, I will lock your ass up!"

"For what? Huh? Can you answer that question sir? I'm not being disrespectful, could you please tell me what for?" as Kelly-Boy held his hands up like if he was pleading for a better understanding.

The Detective watched Kelly and knew that he didn't want to go to jail. But what the Homicide Detective figured thus far was that Kelly knew a lot more then he was telling him. Detective Cooly had been around for many years on the force and knew how some guys dug their own hole, but this guy here was determined to stand on what his mind was already set on.

"Son, there is something you're not telling me, and I'm just going let you know this is never over with because I'll be on you until we figure out why your friend died.

"I don't know anything! And if I did, I still wouldn't be certain if I'll tell you, I'm just being honest."

"Get your ass out of here. I'm pretty sure you can find your own ride?" Cooly said as he looked Kelly-Boy up and down.

"I don't have no problem with that!"

Kelly-Boy's heart was racing and filled with the relief that he felt as he walked out the door.

Kelly-Boy knew there was nothing Wet could say to incriminate him when he knew nothing. Kelly dialed his woman to have her come and pick him up.

"Red" showed up driving her $58,000.00 car. They left heading down the Boulevard.

"What happened, Kelly?" Red asked.

"You know better than to ask me about my business; just drive Bitch!"

"What! You going to handle me like that?"

"Bitch like I said, I'm fucking you! You ain't fucking me and if I'm not doing it right then you need to burn the script up! Now what?" Kelly-Boy said blinking his eyes taking his frustration out on Red's high-dollar ass.

Red drove with her lips poked out and not once did she even think if it was safe for her to respond to Kelly-Boy. She felt like a piece of change that was given to the offering.

Finally pulling in townhouse, Kelly sat in the car waiting for Red to disappear. He watched how she moved. It was a seductive view of what he might not be getting.

Kelly kept dialing Wet's number, but he never picked up. Kelly-Boy sat-there in silence as his mind raced, wondering what the fuck Wet was saying to the cops. His last option was to call Dirty and get a better understanding of what was happening.

Then Kelly thought, Dirty might want to know if they got at old girl. Whatever beef Dirty had with her, he was on his own.

CHAPTER 39 - JUSTINE AND MURK

"C'mon baby, let's go! Lock the house up and let's get out!" Murk said all hysterical and overwhelmed with the murder that just happened.

"What's wrong Murk!? What did you do to dude?" Justine asked, wanting to know as she was panicking.

"I dropped him off at the hospital, now stop asking questions, and come on."

Murk and Justine pulled out of the drive-way and decided to check into a hotel. Murk thought it wasn't his job to gather the cocaine that was possibly scattered all over the Queen City by now.

"What's up Murk? What did they want?" Justine asked.

"C'mon, don't be so naive, they were trying to take you out for that dirty ass police! Don't get soft on me now. I need a gangster bitch, not somebody I need to babysit. I want this shit over just as fast as you do."

"What do you need for me to do?"

"Shit! Do what you do best; I assume that's fucking?"

"Why you say that?"

"I said I assumed. The way you cater to my dick, I figure that was a occupation for you."

"Nah! I'm sorry but you got me confused with the hoes you're probably fucking!" Justine replied now aware of the situation and who her father left at her house. She knew and felt it inside of her veins that she was just the guide stick to get back her father's dope.

"You know your father said you had a way of picking your men, and not yet have one of them that he ever met been his cup of tea. Have you ever just tried black coffee Justine, instead of just sucking out the cream dry?"

Justine now was trapped in a maze with so many ways to follow, but little sense of direction to get where she needed to go. She wanted this to be over just as bad as he did. She now saw a different side of Murk, and it was a cold and lonely place.

They pulled in at the Holiday Inn on Sugar Creek Rd. Murk gathered their things and went inside as he used one of his fake I.D's to purchase the room. Murk walked behind Justine out the front entrance and down the sidewalk until they approached their room which was located on the top stairwell. Murk liked the view from the top were he could see everything that came his way. It was 4:15 in the morning. He had purchased a single bed. "Go ahead and get you a shower, I like it when a woman smells clean; it turns me on," he said as he grabbed her chin roughly.

"I don't like this any more than you do sweetie, we have a job to handle and until we do, you are a part of the problem. Your father made it clear that you will make my stay convenient and you will cater to my needs. It's nothing personal it's just business, now go get your ass in the shower." He said with a smirk on his face like nothing came between him and his decisions.

Justine felt like a slave. She once was willing to give the nigga the pussy, but now she felt horrible, deceived and left hung out to dry. A world only existed for those who wanted to be a part of it, and Justine felt her life depended on the drugs making it back safe.

The water splashed her smooth skin, not a scar anywhere on her body. The water rolled off her shoulders down her chest and over the long nipples on her breasts. She now expressed the falling tears that ran along with the water that ran to the bottom of the tub into the drain where everything disappeared, leaving no trace or indication of her crying or what she felt.

After she was done Justine got out of the shower and dried off, and put her bra and thong on with her hair lose and wet hanging below her shoulders. Tired, but no longer confused, she pulled back the sheets as Murk cleared his gun as he'd portrayed to be this killer that she knew he was.

Justine turned on her side with her back facing him.

Murk was removing his shoes and starting to get comfortable with himself. The message he had left there in Kelly-Boy's yard was a prime example what he was about. Murk knew those guys were far out of their league fucking with him.

Murk slid between the sheets as he heard the heavy breathing that Justine was content with herself. He grabbed the side of her thong and with a hard pull, snatched it off of her ass. He posted up behind her adjusting his dick head between her butt cheeks to get to her dry pussy. His dick sunk in partially, just enough to see him through. Justine still laid on her side as Murk had the rotation now at a speed were they laid silent and listening to wet smacking sounds that echoed throughout the room. The pussy had gotten wetter as Murk penetrated her without a rubber, lifting one side of her ass-cheeks so he was able to get up in her deeper.

CHAPTER 40 - AT WORK

Dirty now was on his way to meet Kingston at the storage facility, driving his police cruiser. He did not yet know about the shooting last night in Hidden Valley.

He pushed the code to get through the gate of the storage facility and drove around to the back where Kingston was parked backward up to the garage door. Kingston looked if he was busy doing something.

"What's up Kingston?" Dirty said, anticipating the money that he was about to get.

"Ain't shit! You got some more of the same packages with the seal on it?" When Dirty looked puzzled, Kingston said, "The dope! It's A-one!"

"The dope's straight! That's all you need to worry about. Is there any reason why I shouldn't trust you?"

"Why? Because I asked you whether the dope was good or not!?"

"You just spooked me asking about the damn seal. What's that got to do with the dope?" Asked Dirty.

"I'm hoping it's coming from the same muthafucker that's all. If you know anything about dope you know that this batch can be good and the next one you got niggas blowing your phone up wanting a refund. That's all I'm saying dawg," he replied, being sure of himself."

"Dawg? What happened to po po? Just cut to the chase, where is my money at?"

Kingston walked in the storage room door where it was connected with other rooms. Dirty watched him very close not knowing what to expect; after all, he was a police.

Kingston returned with a brown paper bag and set it in the trunk of his car. Dirty stood to the side and waited for Kingston to get out of the way.

"It looks like it all might be here but I don't have time to count it. In the mean time, I'll take this bag and put it in my possession. I'll get back to you later on today."

"Yeah, alright!" Said Kingston.

"How did you get rid of the dope so fast?"

"I'm connected in more ways than just fucking with you. Business has got to continue to move on in order to make it happen, as long as I'm not put on hold."

"Give me a few Kingston! There's a lot of business we've got to take care of."

Dirty pulled out from where he could see in his review mirror watching Kingston as he drove away. Dirty knew by his instinct that he and Kingston were going to have a long-term relationship doing business.

Time was pushing and Dirty was running a little late getting to the Police Precinct; it was 6:30 in the morning. Dirty stopped, and put the drug money in his trunk until he felt safe taking it home.

After arriving at the precinct Dirty made a cup of coffee extra sweet like he liked it. Then before he could sit down one of his colleagues walked in his direction and said, "You know the damndest thing happened this morning while I was driving to work!" The Officer said.

"'What?" Dirty asked, waiting on the conversation and sipping hot coffee.

"A deer ran in front of my truck! I hit it, and I knew I had run a part of him over. I got out, and looked at the front of my truck, then thought I would just throw the deer in the bed of my truck. What scared me almost the death was he picked his head and neck up and looked at me. So I jumped back because you know they have hooves sharp enough to cut you in half, if they kick you."

"I didn't know that!" Dirty replied.

"Yeah, yeah! And guess what? The dear got up on his four legs and ran back through the fucking woods!"

"Are you serious?" Dirty said, looking puzzled

"You're damn right I'm serious! I started to shoot it. That's what I should've done," The officer said, like he was upset.

"Why! The beauty of it all was that he still lived."

"Fuck that! Someone called in with the description of my truck and said it was a hit and run, now I'm being relieved from duties pending investigation," Smiley said, leaving out the door.

It's a lot of things been happening with Smiley since his wife left him.

"Carlos! Come here please," the chief said pointing for him to get there."

"Yeah! What's up Chief?" Dirty said, hoping it wasn't nothing about J.J.'s death.

"It was a shooting last night on Bilmark where you busted that house, and dropped charges on them guys. If they are some kind of source you have for information, find out who dropped a person off in front of a crack house, then shot and killed him after letting him out the car. I figured there was a reason you dropped the charges?"

"I'm on it Chief; I do have a few informants there at that spot."

"The sooner the better son."

Dirty felt somebody could tell him something because right now the Chief knew about the charges being dismissed and it was hard to tell what else he might know.

Dirty strolled through his computer, and read the report of the shooting. He saw the victim's face; it was Swig, the same guy that went on the robbery with Kelly-Boy the night when Pat-Rat was killed. He dialed Kelly-Boy's number and it went straight to his voice messages.

Riding through Bilmark, he came to the house and pulled to the curb as he watched crack-heads walk through like it was a parade line.

CHAPTER 41 - CRIME SCENE

"Yo! Come here!" Dirty said to a crack-head that looked like sleep wasn't an option for him.

"What's up?"

"What happened here last night?"

"Hell! I don't know shit; the spot wasn't even open last night."

"You can't tell me they weren't open for business?"

"Police, I can't stand here and talk to you."

Then another crack-head bitch walked by and Dirty said, "Bring your ass here!"

"What?" she said walking up to Dirty real slow.

Dirty thought this was crazy, and he walked up on the spot where they had chalked off where the body and the blood stained the grass.

Dirty needed answers for his Chief, and surely he was thinking Kelly-Boy would be able to make it a whole lot easier. Dirty left and decided to give Kelly-Boy another phone call. He couldn't believe his gold teeth mouth didn't have enough audacity to call Dirty.

Time was ticking away when Dirty left heading to Sugar Creek Rd. when he received an emergency call.

(911 DISPATCH)

"There has been a disturbance at the Holiday Inn where the suspect has broken out a window of a car in the parking lot."

"Copy! I'm on the way."

Dirty was just three minutes away from the hotel.

When he arrived he pulled into the parking lot at the front of the hotel. He saw a couple who were standing beside each other.

Dirty got out of his cruiser, not realizing that the car he was standing in front of with the passenger side window knocked out belonged to Justine. And the couple was her and a stranger.

Dirty caught a glimpse as Justine whispered something in the man's ear. The man stood face to face with Dirty and said, "Officer where are y'all when we really need you?" Murk asked with his eyes locked on Dirty's face like he would never ever forget what he looked like.

"Well sir, it's really hard to be at two places at one time - oh shit, I'm sorry, is that you Justine?" Dirty said, concerned, and trying to see Justine's eyes.

"She's fine officer, what you need to be worrying about is this damn car." Already Murk was hip to Dirty.

"Sir! I'ma ask you to control the tone in your voice."

"I can say what I want officer! The last time I checked we had the freedom of speech?"

"Yeah! But all the disrespecting is not necessary." Dirty replied, looking at the man he didn't know and thinking he was just a man who Justine was letting put his dick in her mouth.

"Only if you knew the definition of respect," Murk said, making the situation personal. He thought if there wasn't so many people watching Murk would have killed Dirty right then in a blink of an eye and then spit in his face.

Dirty was now feeling more of the vibe after talking to this dick-head son-of-bitch. He was thinking the opposite of what Murk had thought, if it was left to Dirty this man that stood in front of him would be a damn dead nigga.

As Dirty walked to peep inside the car, he noticed dried blood stains brushed up against the inside door of the passenger side. Then Murk interrupted and said to Dirty, "Officer like I said you showed up a little late to be of any assistance to us. Besides, we didn't call you! I think the owner did. But me and my woman, we'll get this fixed, so thanks for nothing! C'mon baby!"

"Hey, Justine! Take care. I'll see you around. Maybe at the last place we were alone, remember?" Dirty said as he walked away.

Justine stared Dirty in his eyes, and only if he knew his life had a calling, they pulled off.

Dirty at some point and time felt at ease with the chemistry between him and Justine, but what was difficult for him to read is what did she really know about Dirty's business?

Dirty figured Kingston had been waiting too long so he decided to drop by his house and pick up eight more kilos.

After Dirty pulled in the driveway he went inside and gathered the drugs and put them in two separate boxes, and put his money inside the safe. Sophelia was gone, nowhere to be found.

Dirty left with the boxes in the trunk of his police car, and thought what better way to travel than with drugs. Once again Dirty dialed Kelly Boy's number, but this time he decided to pick up. "Yeah? I'm done fucking with you man, what the fuck you got going on?" Kelly-Boy screamed.

"Calm your ass down nigga! Don't call me crying from a bad dream you done had, faggot!"

"What!"

"Faggot! You heard what the fuck I said, now what the fuck are you talking about boy?"

"Hold up! What's up with all this name-calling Pig?! That's a good name for y'all cops, you greedy ass mutherfucker!"

"You are talking a lot of shit to be living in a hood; and in a crack-house at that!."

"Now I guess you threatening me right?" Kelly-Boy waited for an answer.

"Muthafucker you are my last worry. Tell me what's up with Justine? I just saw the trick with some nigga at the hotel."

"What! What hotel? I'ma kill that muthafucker!"

CHAPTER 42 - DROP OFF

Kelly-Boy wasn't going to do shit. He was happy that it wasn't him that got shot.

"Look let's meet somewhere like in 45 minutes," Dirty said, interested to hear what Kelly-Boy was saying.

"Where man? 'Cause you got a lot of shit with you, I can't trust you by myself, I'm just being real!"

"I'll tell your scared ass what, meet me at I-Hop on W.T Harris, order and I'll pay for it."

"I might bring my bitch!"

"Bring your mom, scared ass nigga!" Dirty said, hanging up.

Dirty now was at the gates of the storage room when he dialed Kingston.

"What's up?" Kingston said.

"I'm here at the spot!" Dirty replied, hanging up. He knew not to talk reckless on his phone.

Kingston was now coming around the corner.

Quickly they made their transaction, limiting their conversation.

Dirty left the storage facility and headed to the I-Hop. He decided to call Kelly-Boy who picked up immediately, and said, "What's up?"

"Where you at?"

"I'm here."

"You bring your family?"

"Nah! But I brought a big ass gun!" click.

Dirty pulled in the parking lot looking for the Chevy but it wasn't nowhere to be spotted. He parked his cruiser; dressed in full uniform, he walked in.

Kelly-Boy was sitting at the table with his back turned. Dirty could spot him a mile away with his little tiny head. Dirty went to sit down, when Kelly screamed.

"Man! What the fuck you doing with that cop suit on, have you lost your damn mind?" Kelly said, looking around to see who was looking. Wasn't anybody paying them any attention but his paranoia.

"Because I am a cop!"

"A damn dirty one!"

"What the fuck you say? Relax Nigga! I'm just fucking with you, where's your sense of humor?"

"Look here man!" Kelly said, watching to see who was looking when he spotted this old lady about 78 years old whispering to her daughter about something that didn't even concern him or Dirty.

"Wait! That old lady watching us; damn man!"

"Nigga! If you don't relax I'ma shoot you my damn self, them people don't know what the fuck our conversation is about you crazy muthafucker."

"Hey Man! That's the last time I'ma be your muthafucker and shit."

Dirty now was laughing so hard inside with this clown being so paranoid. Dirty was a lot bigger then Kelly-Boy when Dirty hauled off and kicked Kelly in his shin.

"Ouch!!! Man, what the fuck are you doing! Son-of-bitch!" He said rubbing his leg.

"Look you wasting my time stop your foolishness and tell me about something I'm missing!"

"Man, that dude killed Swig early this morning," said Kelly-Boy, "man I'll beat your ass if you kick me like that again."

Dirty faked like he was going to kick; they looked like little kids over there playing, when Kelly was mad as hell.

"You kick your damn dog muthafucker! I'm leaving."

"Hold up! Seriously I'll give you two kilos for this information,"

"This muthafucker looked at me like I was next. You took their drugs, and they're not going to get any sleep until they get it back."

"I suggest that you hide!" Dirty said.

"I'll take off and go back home!"

"You are more tied up in this shit then me."

"How you figure?"

"I'm just fucking with you!"

"Look here man! I'm not ready to die, and I ain't got shit to do with it!" Kelly said with determination.

"They are after you dude!"

"How come you say that?"

It started with eight kilos."

"Man if he wanted to do something about that he could've already done it."

"He was fucking your bitch!" Said Dirty.

"That's a damn lie! Shit I know better."

"I shouldn't give you shit! Especially since you sent rookies to go do a professional job."

"Well you should've went and done it your damn self then."

"I might just do that, and you better hope I get the job done because you are in it just as deep."

"What about the two kilos?"

"Nigga you better feel lucky I don't slap the shit out of you after that story."

Dirty walked out and Kelly-Boy was so mad he wanted to kill his ass. Kelly left his potatoes, steak, and eggs as Dirty fucked his appetite up.

CHAPTER 43 - PENTHOUSE

Today was voluntary for the girls, but this particular day Regina didn't have a choice. They decided to check out a few bars.

They arrived uptown and the sight was beautiful; the lights were bright and people were coming and going. They passed a club on College Street called "Cosmos" where they have a mechanical bucking bull that couples enjoy riding.

It was 1:30 a.m and they decided to go inside. The girls were dressed so fly no one could notice that they were some straight hoes who would take them green bills for a ride for their money.

Surrounding them were mostly college students who drank Tequila, and sucked on lemon lime.

"Hey, Girl! Look at that fine boy checking you out Regina," CeCe said still cheesing because Regina had to be at least 15 years older than him even though she didn't look it.

"He is way too young!" Regina replied, trying to avoid looking his way. She didn't want to entice him any more then she already had.

"Can you believe this shit? Oh my God! Tell me he's not coming over here," Regina said.

"Excuse me! Hey you! Excuse me!" the young guy yelled, as Regina acted if the music was too loud and she couldn't hear anything he was saying.

Regina was close enough where she had a perfect look at his young face, she still could see the peach fuzz hairs on his face that hadn't yet turned black.

Then all of a sudden he whispered into Regina's ear and said, "Can I have a moment by myself with you on the dance floor?"

"How you figure we'll be by ourselves?" Regina shot back without looking him in his baby face.

"At least out in the open everyone can see I'm with the baddest thing in here!" The young stud replied.

"I don't even know your name?"

"De'Angelo!"

"I tell you what; buy me Tequila and we can dance all night."

"Okay! Hold on, I'll be back!"

"Oh no! Is that how you do it?" Regina said.

"What?" he asked, wondering what she was talking about?

"You just going to leave me here for somebody else to pull the baddest thing in here?"

"Hmmm, come on baby."

As De'Angelo passed, some of the guys he knew were checking him out walking with Regina. She looked nothing like a crack-head, she had some of the most beautiful skin with her mini skirt hugging on her thighs, her muscle showed with each step she took, while her butt cheeks flexed, and she was dressed to kill.

By this time they reached the bar, and De'Angelo ordered their drinks when the bartender said, "I.D please!"

De'Angelo pulled out a $50 dollar bill trying to hand it to him looking over at Regina cheesing.

"Sir! I.D."

"Wait! I must have left it in the car."

"I'm sorry; try a better one than that, because everyone needs an I.D to get in the club."

The bartender took the drink back, and then Regina threw all five fingers in his face, and left him standing there.

Monica and CeCe were on the dance floor jamming with some young kids.

Then she heard a whisper in her ear, "Damn Baby! Why you give up on me so fast? Here goes your drink," De'Angelo tried to hand it to Regina.

"I know you better get rid of it before you go to jail."

"How? Ain't no police around Baby; here take it."

"I'm a Cop!" Regina replied lying through her teeth.

You should've seen Casanova turn the corner and she didn't care if he spread lies on her because she didn't see anyone of interest. The music was loud and Monica was in the Doggy Style position while this young dude grinded on her old ass. Regina thought there were better places she could've been with a glass dick (crack pip) in her mouth.

Finally after the song was through playing they both came over where Regina stood and said, "What! Shit we was going to ask them to get a hotel room," CeCe said.

"That just did it! Young ass boys, you absolutely right, he couldn't even buy alcohol, when I left him he came back with the drinks and I told him I was a Police! I haven't seen him since.

"Damn! Come on lets go before the boys think we police for real," Monica said.

Not wasting any time they left the club heading back to the car to go home.

CHAPTER 44 - JUSTINE AND MURK

Murk had Justine's car on fire, burning it to a crisp as the black smoke raised high in the sky. Now they were driving a car Murk had rented using one of his fake I.D's.

Justine sat on the passenger side looking like she was being abused and couldn't all the way pull it together. She thought how Murk was just a hard core dude who did exactly what he wanted to. A plea bargain wasn't even an option. The more time she spent with him the more she learned about him personally.

This was one of those tragic moments when Justine felt that the dope was more important than her; she was just a small fraction to what was really going on.

"Your father claims you have a history of fucking police officers, I mean he told me about the one that was killed but what about this one, did you fuck him too?" Murk asked being straight forward about the question.

"Yeah! I do have a history of fucking me a dick that's worth riding. Oh! Did I fuck that cop? Yeah I did. He bent me over a truck seat and fucked me good and hard like I like it."

"Damn! You good-pussy bitch! But it didn't surprise me at all, I could put your ass on a hoe stroll to make some money to get groceries, you really not worth much; cheap ass hoe," he said.

He was now driving along the neighborhood trying to remember how to get back to Bilmark, traveling Tom Hunter Rd.

"Justine, you opened a can of worms and they have spread everywhere. This is a disposition for your father. Where is the money your boyfriend had to back the dope up, so we can call off this man hunt. Oh yeah! That cop has made this personal between me and him. Just imagine if I wasn't there at your house, you would've been dead. That's how much the police care about you. Ain't that some shit! You fucked him with the dick that was worth riding, now he's ready to kill your ass. It's some shit that you got to understand about life and why I'm like I am."

"I don't want to hear that shit! Sometimes you are this charming, and affectionate type of dude and next you make a bitch feel like she don't wanna be around you."

"That's what I'm talking about right there. You know what to expect from a nigga 'cause I'm subject to take your ass out at any given time. Life is business, and not affectionate.

Murk passed the house that appeared to be where he shot and killed Dude. He drove up and down the street about four times. People walked the streets here at night like it was a block party. But nigga's were getting money.

"Get out!" Murk said.

"For what?" she screamed.

"Find that nigga, the one that stays at that house, we passed it about three times; mangle with the crack-heads and ask questions - fuck if you have too. You got my number if you need me.

THE HOOD IN HIDDEN VALLEY

Justine was put out of the car and she walked in the direction of the trap house. Crack-heads went in and out. Wet appeared on the porch.

"Yo, Shorty!" Wet yelled as she kept walking, not trying to get herself killed and not knowing who knew her. Justine stopped just a little bit past the house.

"Hold up Baby!" Wet said, running off the porch cheesing like a cat.

"What's your name?"

"Janet!"

"You stay around here?"

"Nah! Countryside Apts."

"You walking by yourself, I Mean where you coming from?" Wet asked like he was concerned.

"You sure are asking a lot of questions."

"I mean it's late, and as fine as you are I wouldn't want anything to happen to you; can a brother be concerned?"

"I suppose so, where you live?" Justine asked looking into Wet's face, and she thought how good looking he was.

"On Snow White, right down this street a little, this is just our trap house. It belongs to me and my nigga."

"Don't use that word, I can't stand it, it's not cute."

"Oh, I'm sorry! Mine and Kelly-Boy's."

Justine and Wet stood there a little just talking as Murk drove by a few times observing the area. She really liked Wet and thought there was something different about him from any of the other brothers she ever put time into. They traded numbers and said their goodbyes.

"You sure you don't want me to walk you half-way? I can Janet!"

"I wouldn't want to stop you from getting money! Because if you go with me you will be going a lot farther than half way; like all the way," she said giving Wet a sexy smile and twisting her petite ass.

After she was out of sight Murk pulled up, and Justine got in the car. She sat there on the passenger side and looked straight ahead knowing that Murk wouldn't have any compassion for Wet. She would be the blame for everything that was going on.

"Who was old boy," Murk asked.

"One of Kelly-Boy's workers."

"So that's his name, Kelly-Boy?"

"Yeah"

"You get old boy's number?"

Justine paused before giving any feedback to him. She gave Murk the idea that she didn't want to answer.

"Yeah!"

"Damn girl! The little talking we did didn't do you any good at all. Your little panties got wet. This here is serious; put my dick down your throat and get off his. People about to lose their lives. You better wake your ass up! Fuck babysitting."

CHAPTER 45 - DIRTY

It was Early Morning, and Dirty was off duty today.

He left Sophelia there in the bed, and thought he would do some observation and ride around the Queen City, and put his foot in the shoes of his killer.

Dirty couldn't quite pen point nothing at the moment, but who in their right mind would kill a Cop other than with his authorization besides a muthafucker that's almost missing a hundred kilos. Dirty went into a deep thought when it occurred they could be close like parked at the Police station watching Dirty come and go.

He knew it wouldn't be on debating, if Dirty were anywhere close he would kill'em. Damn Dirty couldn't kick the thought that his life was on the line and didn't know which direction they were coming. Should he make his wife and son leave until this was over? Never did Dirty see himself in a situation where the shoes now felt like they were on the other foot. But what he refused to do is let some local hit man take him out.

Dirty was now riding pass his Penthouse and no one appeared to be up, there sitting in the parking lot was Monica car.

So Dirty decided to pull in and sat in his truck. "Damn! I wonder if Kelly-Boy will answer his phone, Dirty said out loud not really having a friend to turn too, something that he said he didn't need.

Especially after threatening Kelly-Boy the way he did. Dirty decided to try his luck. The phone rang multiple times then he answered.

"What man? Why the fuck are you calling me, huh? Whatcha you want," Kelly asked like he was frustrated.

"Look Kelly-Boy, I'm off work lets meet somewhere so we can talk.

"Man!!! Is you crazy! I just look like this. Anything you want to tell me, say it on the phone, fuck that."

"Ha, Ha, ha."

"What the fuck's funny? Tell me so I can laugh, too."

"You a damn trip! But before I do, I swear it's something bothering me about this situation that we-talked about before.

"Look man! I really want my shit you owe me, when am I gonna get it, huh?. Swig was killed yesterday, and I broke into his Girlfriend house looking for his dope."

"Damn Kelly! He's suppose to be your friend?"

"Yeah! But what a dead man going to do with it huh?."

"I could've drawn up a search warrant, and went and got it for you?"

"Noooo...., hell no! So you could keep it."

"Ha, ha, ha," Dirty laughed. "You think I'm playing, you would've got it."

They chopped it up for a little more when Dirty realized that he didn't have a friend in the world, but his wife, and he was trying hard to keep that dick in her ass.

It was something about I-Hop where Dirty and Kelly were on their way to. Kelly-Boy wouldn't get caught nowhere else with him besides a public place.

Dirty was already there when his phone rang, he looked at it and Sophelia was calling.

"Hey Honey! What's wrong?"

"Nothing, I just called when I saw that you were gone. I just wanted to tell you that I love you. I thought this was your day off?"

"Baby it is, I had to meet with a friend here at the I-Hop down the street from the house, are you hungry?, do you want me to order you something?"

"Please do! Can I ride through and pick it up?"

"I don't see why you can't, C'mon it's waiting for you."

"Okay honey give me a moment to get myself together, I love you Sophelia said."

"I love you, too!" Dirty said hanging the phone up when he heard a voice say, "I love you, Baby."

"Sat your ass down, Kelly!"

"Look! Before I do, muthafucker you kicked me, will fighting!"

"Look Kelly, you just don't know how happy I am to see you.

"O yeah!!!! You ain't got your Cop suit on, I'll beat your ass!

Funny muthafucker Dirty thought. Time was limited, it wouldn't take long for his wife to get there, he ordered Sophelia's food and then Kelly and Dirty ordered their food and got comfortable.

"What you got to tell me that you couldn't tell me on the phone?" Kelly asked.

"I didn't tell you that I had looked the dude in the eyes before I knew he killed your boy. And the thing about it, he's not after you, it's me! Y'all just got caught up at the wrong place at the wrong time.

"I…I didn't even care how he shot him. After we heard the shots, we turned and ran back through the house and jumped over the neighbor's back fence. He delivered a message that he meant business!" Kelly expressed with a facial expression that he was more scared now than ever.

"Hello, Honey! Sophelia said interrupting their conversation.

"Oh! Hey baby."

"Kelly-Boy, this is my wife Sophelia, Sophelia Kelly."

"Darn, you bad," Kelly said as he reached out to grab her hand.

The waitress brought her food and Dirty walked his wife to the door.

"Damn, she's bad!" Kelly said again."

"I don't need you to remind me how bad my wife is."

"I bet you would kill a nigga for trying to fuck with her?"

For a moment Dirty didn't say shit as the thought hit him.

"We need to stay focused on the nigga who's trying to kill us!"

"Ooooo... you scared now?"

"Far from it, I just need you to give me a better understanding.

"On what, ol' boy? Yeah, he's a killer; most definitely. But you so damn dirty, we can't help each other. But at the end, I'ma dead nigga."

"Why you say that?"

"Because you gonna kill me. I no longer have anything to do with it. Just give me what you promised."

Dirty knew inside that something was keeping him from being open and more direct about the whole matter. Kelly was looking for any kinda help to make a come up. Kelly thought small and his brains weren't big enough to elevate to another level. So Dirty decided to do himself a favor and leave him in the hood with little success thinking he would ever be able to come out and see his accomplishment. But it would be the same for him re-up after re-up until someone stopped him in his footsteps.

Dirty knew major money for and average nigga that lived in the hood and watching behind his own back every second of the day was more sweat than he could ever bear. You're only as big as your dream could be. And actual reality it's a struggle to keep it alive.

CHAPTER 46 - FEW WEEKS PASS

Thursday night and Justine now had set a date up with Wet. Murk and Justine were in the hotel that set off from Independence Boulevard. Murk was ready to nip all this bullshit in the bud. He knew this had been going on for far too long. When a man weakness was a woman, next thing to money was a nut.

"Look, Justine! Call your boy and tell him that your girlfriend came out at the last minute and see if Kelly-Boy will come to accompany her. Sell the story. If you don't, then you will have to get at him another time," Murk said looking at her. "Go ahead, Bitch! I'm not playing with you, I'll blow your ass out that chair just as you sit with this 10 meter Miller and tell your father a lie why I had to. Do I make myself clear?"

"Yeah!"

"Wait! Get your thoughts together before picking up that phone. I'm tired now because I haven't killed me uh muthafucker, don't you be the one."

Words that had been spoken and she wasn't ready to die. "I'm sorry Murk! They didn't show any compassion when they kicked through my door trying to take my life, so I don't understand why I should show any sympathy." Justine said, really not meaning what she said but trying to comfort Murk because she believed Murk was ready to kill her.

"Make the call since you feeling like that, make it happen." He said with this look she didn't want to remember."

Justine grabbed her cell phone thinking a million things, hoping Wet didn't answer the phone, especially when she knew his face didn't look familiar from the previous home invasion. How could she witness an innocent person die because of her. This time she thought, if she had that gun, he would be dead.

"Hello! Hmmmm.... Wet? Damn, I hate to break you the bad news, player."

"Oh no! What's the reason sweetie...please don't tell me, call the sheriff and tell him that I just got shot down and the bullet is in my heart."

"You are stupid! My girlfriend just came in town and she wants to go out as well. And, she don't have nobody."

"She can come along with us! I'm pretty sure you're more than enough woman for me, baby! Please, I beg you don't do me like this," Wet said as if this was the biggest disappointment of his life.

"What about Kelly-Boy? Your friend?"

"Let me call him. I'll call you right back. Okay, baby?"

"Alright, bye!"

"See, how easy that was?" Murk said cleaning his gun.

Time passed and no phone call.

Murk paced the floor and was curious if Kelly-Boy was even smart enough to even have a hint when his boy was over excited and thinking with his dick.

"C'mon let's ride! I'll have some results for your father before the night is over."

"Where we goin?"

"Stop asking all these questions and bring your ass on."

Leaving the hotel and onto Independence Boulevard, Murk grabbed his cell and dialed a number. The call went straight to voice mail.

Now, Murk was boiling hot.

Traveling at a speed of 97 mph when Justine asked, "Why are you speeding?"

"Shut your fucking mouth, bitch! I'm only 5 seconds from making you lose your life."

"I haven't done nothing!" She started crying.

"Shut up and turn your fucking phone on, trick!"

Justine thought this dude was too true to be real. He had picked a hold card that she used to try and save Wet's life. When she pushed the button to turn the phone back on, it started beeping.

"Good God!" Murk said as he snatched it out her hand.

"What's the code? What is it?" he said as his face changed to different facial expression. You could see the rage that he wanted to kill.

Murk dialed the code and this is what one of the 9 messages that was still left had to say.

"What's up, Baby? This Wet, Kelly-Boy and me are together as I speak, where is your location? Hit us back."

Murk had it on the loud speaker.

"Call them back! Here!"

Quickly Justine dialed the number.

"Yeah! What's up? We're together baby! Which Hotel?" Wet asked happy that she returned the call.

Justine took the time out to give Wet directions to her location she told them she had to go pick up her girlfriend and that she would be back momentary.

Murk listened to the conversation and thought finally how he approved of Justine's unacceptable behavior when he only wanted to do was get down to the bottom when he still felt like he was at the top and hadn't accomplished shit.

Justine was having the feeling about a thug on the streets, and seriously didn't know the severity between life and death. And the games she chose to play.

CHAPTER 47 - HOTEL

"I'm telling you, if she's ugly I'm out. She's got to look at least close enough to my bitch. If not I'm out, because I can be home fucking mine. You feel me?"

Kelly-Boy and Wet sat in the parking lot that was packed with other cars. Kelly-Boy had to show that he was a dope boy sitting in his Chevy Caprice on 26 inch rims looking down on anything that came, his way.

"C'mon Kelly, let's get out and stunt on these hoes!" Wet said excited ready to fuck Justine.

"Hell no! I got my jewelry on and ain't no telling where the Jack boys are at, especially how I'm sitting pretty! Just set back partner and let them hoes come to us."

After about five minutes, a car pulled in the hotel parking lot, driving slow as if they were looking at every vehicle that was parked on the premises.

"That might be them. Let me wave them down," Wet said.

"Wait! It's a dude driving that car. That can't be them. Just chill and sit back. If she's ugly, I'm telling you dawg I'm pulling out, ain't no secret."

"Man, I'll bet you she's bad! What you want to bet on it?"

"All your week's earnings. You sure you want to do that?" Kelly-Boy looked at Wet not hesitant about the handshake to cover the bet.

"Man that is her getting out that car! That's Janet." Wet said trying to open the car door on his side.

"Wait! Get your ass back in here! That's the bitch we're supposed to kill! Get in and close the door," Kelly said ducking in his seat trying to avoid being seen.

"Are you sure?"

"Fuck yes I'm sure! Luckily she didn't see you. We've got to get out of here." Kelly said shaking. They had a prefect view of Justine walking on the top part of the steps and the car went down in the flat and parked.

Then Wet's phone rang. It was Justine.

No, don't answer yet! Wait a minute. Tell her we went to the store and we will be right back. Do you hear me?"

"Yeah!" Wet replied.

Finally, Wet answered the phone. "What's up baby?"

"Please! I don't know what to do, he's trying to kill y'all and if I don't get you up here, I'm dead!" she cried.

"We're in the parking lot, run!"

"Shut up fool. Are you crazy?" Kelly-Boy screamed looking in the direction where the car had parked.

"I can't. If I come back out of this room, I'm dead." Justine cried not wanting to be a part of this shit any longer.

"What's going on?" Kelly-boy asked in the back ground.

"Look, Janet. ..."

"No, my name is Justine!"

"I'm already hip, he parked almost down on the end. Is there any way you can get out?" Wet asked.

"No! I'm facing him. If that door comes open, he said it better be for y'all."

"Okay, okay, stop crying, hold on for a minute."

"What are we going to do, Kelly?"

"What? We're leaving that bitch in there. Shit! I'm not about to die."

"Wait, I'm going in the room to buy some time."

"Are you fucking crazy? You'd better save your own ass!"

"I'm going inside," Wet said not thinking straight.

"Don't let him see you get your ass out of this car," Kelly said not once taking his eyes off dude in the cut. Kelly was starting to sweat.

Wet got out of the car and walked across the lower level and then upstairs.

Kelly was trying to figure out what to do; he knew these folks were serious. Kelly watched as Wet knocked on the door and then looked behind for him.

Kelly-Boy grabbed his cell and dialed Dirty who answered on the first ring.

"What's up?"

"Look here, Dirty. Come quick! My partner is in the room with Justine and dude is sitting in his car down on the other end watching," Kelly said like he was out of breath.

"Where? Where, Kelly?"

"At the Hotel on Independence; across from the cricket arena."

"I'm on my way!" Dirty said hanging up.

Kelly's nerves were bad and he didn't know when dude was going to get out the car at any 'given time. Then, Kelly-Boy's phone rang. "Hello," Kelly-Boy said real low as if he was trying not to let anyone hear him, other than the caller. It was Wet.

"Kelly," Justine called him and said you were on your way. She bought us a little time to figure out what we need to do."

"Dirty's on his way. If that muthafucker gets out, I'm running his ass over with my car. You are a stupid nigga! All this over a bitch after all that talking and lecturing you gave me, I thought you were smarter than this."

"If you remember my lectures, I'm not about taking anybody's life."

"Just be careful and if I call you, answer that damn phone."

"Okay!"

Kelly-Boy sat so high that be could see everything that moved. He really wanted to know why in the fuck he was still there and what was taking Dirty's ass so long.

Then Kelly noticed the lights come on inside of dude's car. He couldn't see what he was doing when the truck pulled in but it wasn't Dirty, or at least he didn't think so because he couldn't remember his particular truck.

"Fuck! Dude's getting out," Kelly said out loud trying to figure what to do next. Kelly redialed Dirty.

"What's up, Kelly."

"How far away are you man? Dude just got out of his car. Fuck this! I'm gone!!" Kelly screamed.

Boom, boom, boom!

"What the fuck?" Kelly said out loud as he heard the shots close by.

He hit the floor of his car shaking like a leaf.

Devon Sturdivant

CHAPTER 48 - SCENE

Everybody had come out of their hotel rooms to see where the gun fire had come from. Kelly-Boy saw a man lying in the middle of the parking lot. He still had his phone in the palm of his hand and said, "Dirty, Dirty," Kelly whispered into his phone, still ducking in his seat. Nobody answered so Kelly decided to call Wet.

"Hello? Who is that laying in the parking lot?" Wet asked.

"How in the hell do I know? It's dark."

"Bring your ass on or you're left!"

"That muthafucker could be hiding in between these cars."

"Bring your ass on!"

Kelly looked up in the direction of the hotel room when he saw Wet and Justine coming out. Kelly-Boy looked around for any sign of dude; people still were gathered around the body.

"C'mon boy. Get in," Kelly screamed and quickly pulled off.

Now on Independence, Kelly looked at Justine and said, "Man, you about got us killed! I hope she's worth it, nigga."

"Chill out Kelly! She saved our lives!" Wet said with his arm around Justine, who was crying.

"When you tried to take mine, I remember you were with that other guy that killed my boyfriend," Justine said shivering.

Kelly thought how the problem just started and he couldn't figure out how he got mixed in this bullshit. Cocaine was a gold mine to blacks, but the hours and sweat you had to go through to get rid of it, and sometimes in the course of-it all how many lose their lives behind it trying to come up.

Kelly explained how he had called Dirty when he heard the loud gun fire that seemed so close. He thought he heard the gun fire loud and clear from Dirty's phone.

Still late in the morning, Wet decided he wanted to get dropped off along with Justine at his mother's house in the Valley.

Kelly dropped them off then tried to call Dirty. When he didn't get any answer, he left a voice message that said, "Call me!"

MORNING TIME

Dirty pulled out heading to the precinct, never at ease for the simple fact he felt like his business was still in the streets. Dirty knew he didn't have any more use for Kelly-Boy because his life meant more than a friendship, right when he felt Kelly was protecting the bitch that knew more about his business. Just her being alive could put his ass behind bars for life. He wasn't about to let them get ahead.

Turning in the parking lot of the precinct, Dirty walked in and got comfortable at his desk with his hot cup of coffee, and went through a few pieces of paper that were being unattended.

Once he finished, Dirty walked around, and didn't feel any threats or odd chemistry being surrounded with his colleagues. Walking with his head up and very enthusiastic, he left the police precinct.

Dirty was driving down Independence and thought he would ride by the hotel to make sure they chalked off the spot were dude was killed.

Dirty thought how the timing was perfect, and seeing his face Dirty would never forget, like if he was a walking ghost determined to do what he came for!

Pulling in the parking lot, Dirty drove around and just as he thought it was chalked and taped around the crime scene. Dirty kept driving on around and left when he decided to give Kelly-Boy a call back, and see what he knew about last night. After the second ring, Kelly picked up.

"Yo, man! That muthafucker killed somebody last night in the parking lot! I think he probably thought that was me," Kelly sounded like he was just waking up.

Dirty knew Kelly didn't have a clue so he decided to leave him in the dark when Dirty said, "I turned around after I saw a couple of police cars racing in that direction. Shit, to be honest I thought it was a set-up."

"I wouldn't do you like that. I'm real man!"

"Where's the girl?"

"At Wet's house! That nigga risked his own life to save her."

"How did that come about with her in the first place?" Dirty asked real curious.

Dirty listened to Kelly how dude had sent ol' girl to the hood apparently to draw them in, but Wet fell in love at first sight, something that would get him killed later on in the future with the drug game.

Dirty listened to every detail of the situation then came up with the conclusion that Wet was even more of a threat because Wet was able to get everything from the source's mouth, and how he couldn't trust either of the two.

"So they didn't have a clue who that was that got killed in the parking lot?"

"Nope, but after you wouldn't answer your phone I thought you did it because the sound was even louder coming through my phone."

"Ha, ha," Dirty laughed being optimistic.

"What's funny?" Kelly asked.

"How is that possible when I wasn't able to make it?"

"Nothing surprises me with you," Kelly sighed.

"I'll get those kilos for you. When are you ready?"

"I need to get that now! You promised me!"

"Keep your phone on," Dirty said."

CHAPTER 49 - PENTHOUSE

"Ahh... ahhh... ahh... Oh God! Get in me, big daddy, please don't stop... Ahh... ahh... ow... You're hurting me baby... oh shit! Ahh... ahh... That's it. You the man, L.T."

"Damn right, I'm the man in charge! I must admit this is the best piece of ass I've had in a minute, and some very expensive ass, too. How would you like to go home with me and be my wife?" Lieutenant asked, really meaning it.

Regina really put on a show and knew this wasn't the woman she wanted to be in life, fulfilling people's sexual desires like a slut bucket.

"Ahh... ahh... yeah baby! Take me with you. Oh God, you're hurting my butt cheeks... Big Daddy, oh yeah, hit it."

After about two hours, Lieutenant thought how Sophelia just threw him to the wolves and finally he had been bitten, when he thought it was impossible for the hook-up and he owed Sophelia; he knew she would never leave her husband.

Regina walked out the bedroom. CeCe and Monica happened to be sitting in the living room relaxing and talking about the regular routines and how they just got fucked.

L.T was carrying Regina's belongings, following her like a little lost puppy. Regina didn't know how this was supposed to play out, but she was ready to move on and take a chance. She thought about Dirty chasing her around the world just to replace his misfortune. Regina knew she would be irreplaceable to someone who wanted to be here.

CeCe and Monica were content as Regina displayed the reaction on her face that she wasn't to be messed with when she had finally confided within herself.

They hugged and cried with tears that they had developed. Lieutenant made a few trips in and out of the house, taking luggage to the car.

The number one rule was never to interact with a client, but this certain one seemed to have rules of his own.

"Damn CeCe! What are we going to tell Dirty? That she left with a foot soldier and he was armed and dangerous?" Monica said laughing.

"Most definitely not! We tell him that she got caught smoking crack and we felt like the safest thing to do was to kick her out before she became a problem."

"I'm happy for her, girl," Monica said.

"I wonder what the fuck he did differently than any other soldier that came through these doors?"

"It ain't no telling!"

"Well... whatever it was I need to get me one like that," CeCe's little ass said.

* * *

COFFEE SHOP

Dirty and a few other cop were taking their lunch break sitting at the bar drinking some coffee, when one officer they called Pac-Man notified the other officers and said, "You heard what happened last night at the hotel on Independence?" he said while Dirty ear-hustled trying to find out what they knew. The TV news came on in the background.

"This is the 12:00 News. There was a murder that occurred early this morning when a man was shot to his death walking back from his vehicle to his hotel room. More on the 12:00 News when we return."

"Check this out! The guy was sitting in his car and smoked crack all night. He never smoked in the room because his wife forbids it." Pac-Man said.

Then, the other officers listened as Dirty said, "You talk like this was a regular routine for him?"

"Yeah it is because the man that was killed was the maintenance man for the hotel," Pac-Man said.

Dirty thought what the fuck, they didn't know shit! That's what they do when they debate about something, just making speculation. Dirty knew he was the one that killed the muthafucker.

"Whoever shot the crack-head, the muthafucker hit him slap in the heart close range," Pac-Man said.

"Who would want to kill the maintenance man?" the other Cop asked.

"He probably owed every drug dealer who moved dope over there, the place is infested. Muthafuckers don't get any sleep, trust me I know, that's my area."

Dirty laughed inside because he had known Pac-Man for some years and he was close to retiring. He had been on the force forever; almost 35 years. He knew all the "crooked cops" around the force, all the tricks-of-the-trade, but what Dirty was certain about was that Pac-Man didn't have the slightest idea about this one. Pac-Man was the type that wanted to know it all.

Then Dirty looked down at his cell because he had it on vibrate. It was Sophelia.

"Yeah," Dirty said listening.

Dirty wasn't surprised at all that Regina would take flight. He asked Sophelia if she took her last payment and she said no. Dirty knew that every smoker wanted their last paycheck.

After hanging up, the News came back on. Dirty just sat and watched, laughing as the reporters got all the details wrong.

CHAPTER 50 - WET CRIB

"Are you awake, sleepy head?" Justine asked while caressing through Wet dreads.

"Has my mom left for work yet?"

"She has. She's a very nice lady. She told me I was welcome to anything in the house, and what's funny, she said nothing about her son. Ha, ha, ha."

"Well, believe it. What time is it?."

"Hmmm....11:55a.m."

"Did my mom fix breakfast?"

"Oh I see, you're a momma's boy?"

"Boy?!"

"You sure you ain't her man!."

"Damn! That's crazy. That's my mom, crazy girl!"

Justine knew that Wet was real smart and highly intelligent to wanna risk his life to save her's or anyone else's. His thugism was somewhat immature, and not well developed portraying to be somebody that he wasn't. He was caught up in a world of acting and didn't realize that there were real bullets in exchange for a life.

"So do you want to tell me what's going on?" Wet asked looking tired.

"Oh, please don't make me go through this again. I figure your down with the plot from the beginning. Why do you want me to explain something you already know?"

"To be honest, I know only a little, but not the whole story. But it's okay if you don't want to talk about it. I'm not going to force you."

Justine had a thousand things running through her mind. Who was that laying in the parking lot? Was it Murk? And if it was, her Daddy had more men to replace him. It almost seemed like a needle in the haystack for her.

One thing was for sure, she didn't want to mislead Wet thinking there could be something between them. She knew Wet was young and could have a promising life ahead of himself if he thought deep inside what he wanted out of life.

"I'm thinking some sausage, eggs, grits and biscuit with some butter and orange juice. What do you think?"

"Sounds great, but who's going to make all that?"

"What's wrong? You never cooked for your girlfriend before? Or, does your mommy serve you in bed, baby boy?"

"Why do I feel like you ain't feeling me?"

"Well, your feeling is wrong! I'm feeling you too much, that's what's scaring me, pumpkin."

"Oh God! Please don't call me that! My mom used that word all the time."

"How old are you? Nineteen? Twenty?"

"I'm eighteen, but will be nineteen in about six months."

"Do you have a Nextel plug for my phone?" Justine asked.

"Yeah, my mom does. I've got a cricket phone."

She watched Wet get up from the bed with his bird chest. Would she be wrong if she fucked him she thought. Not because she wanted the dick, but because he was her hero. She analyzed the situation and knew she wasn't the bad guy when his friend wanted to take her life. What she wanted to do was get out of this house.

* * *

COFFEE SHOP

"C'mon Dirty! Is that you shitting all over yourself?" Pac-Man asked.

"Nah. That smells like some old shit; can't be anybody but you Pac-Man."

"Ha, ha, ha! Wait gentlemen, the News is back on."

Dirty anticipated seeing who this assassin was and where he was from. Still, what troubled him was Justine wasn't fully in compliance with the hit from what he had gathered from Kelly-Boy.

Finally, the news came on Channel 9. "Hello I'm Jade Sturdivant and we come to you with a murder that occurred late last night in the North Charlotte area. The man was shot close-range in the chest and was killed instantly. All we could gather was that the man was returning to his hotel room. They sent his body for an autopsy and hopefully, later on, we'll have the name."

"There you go, damn sure didn't say shit about a maintenance man smoking crack, Pac-Man," the other officer yelled out.

"They don't know what the fuck they're talking about. I do!"

"Y'all believe that shit if you want to."

"Hey Dirty! You gone?" Pac-Man asked.

"Yeah, I'll see you guys around."

"Okay. Take care and be careful in them streets son," Pac-Man said.

Dirty got in his cruiser. Pac-Man almost had Dirty feeling like he had some doubts about the whole ordeal. But Dirty knew better. He looked Dude in his eyes before he let off the trigger. Now he was going to call Kelly-Boy and let him know where they needed to meet.

"Yeah! What's up, partner?"

'Where do you want to meet?"

"You're asking me?!"

"Don't I always ask your scared ass? I saw on the news your boy was killed."

"He's dead? I'll tell you something. I heard the shots just as loud as if it came out of your phone."

"I believe you're starting to know too damn much!"

"Did you ever stop to think you heard the shot because you were there? Dumb-ass nigga!"

"What's up dawg?"

"Oh. I'm your dawg now? I should shit on you, but I feel like this time you deserve it. I'm on my way to go pick it up."

Click.

Dirty felt good that old boy was finally out of the way. His main concern now was Justine.

CHAPTER 51 - BREAKFAST

After Justine and Wet finished eating their breakfast, Wet went to take a shower, and Justine grabbed her cell phone off the charger. She left and walked down the street and in the process of doing so, she called a taxi. She appreciated everything the young Wet had done for her, but she wished there was something she could truly offer him besides her body.

Coming down the street, the taxi approached her and she flagged it down. Justine thought how she looked a hot mess and needed a hot shower.

"Take me to the Marriott in the University area."

"Are you alright, ma'am?" the taxi driver asked, watching Justine from his rear-view mirror.

"Just mind your business please, and drive."

Justine sat up in her seat and felt more comfortable when the thought hit her that she believed the man that lay in the parking lot was Murk! She never witnessed anyone like him before in her life. She couldn't believe no one had called her yet.

The taxi pulled in to the Marriott and she reached inside of her pocket and paid the driver.

When Justine went to make a call, she noticed her battery was dead. "Fuck!" she said out loud, mad at herself.

After purchasing the room, she caught the elevator up to her room. Once inside, she thought how she would call her father. She didn't want to talk to him right now because Murk had her feeling she was just a number instead of family, so she had to build up enough nerves to accommodate her father. She felt fatigued from the ordeal trying to watch out for her life. Justine decided that she would get some sleep before she called.

***

TRAP HOUSE

"Man, I told you, she's got her tail between her legs. You're still trying to sniff, and she gave you her ass to kiss partner," Kelly-Boy said shaking his head.

"She was scared." Wet said.

"Of what? That bitch is a lot smarter than you think. Now she knows where your black-ass lives. You should've brought that bitch here to the trap house and slept with her.

"She ain't like that; trust me."

"Like what? Help me understand what you're talking about, please!"

"Look, I don't want to talk right now."

"I don't blame you!"

Kelly-Boy thought about how Dirty kept it real and dropped off the two kilos in the police car. Kelly kept watching Wet. He looked like he was sick! Kelly thought how could a bitch make you feel like that when you have never fucked her. Kelly didn't want to tell Wet without touching a feeling inside of him, but he was about to make the same mistake both of his brothers had made that caused them to lose their lives.

If they were anything like Wet, then Kelly could understand. But right now, Kelly knew there was money to be made. He now felt safe because he really had a way to deny it.

"Look here player! Get your ass off those steps and pull yourself together. I'll try and help you get that car," Kelly-Boy said.

"Shit, even the crack-heads haven't come out," Wet replied.

"Hey, Man! You need to come out of it. That girl doesn't care about you."

A car was coming up the street and a female was driving. She stopped right in front of the drive-way. The windows were tinted. Wet's attention was drawn to the girl that was driving the car. He knew that Justine would come back. The window came down all the way on the passenger side.

"Justine?" Wet asked from afar.

"Yeah!"

"Damn girl! I'm glad you came back because this boy has been sick! You hear me?" Kelly-Boy said.

"Yeah, I thought you said she wouldn't come back?"

"She tricked the shit out of me," Kelly said walking to the car. Murk came up from the passenger side. Wet and Kelly were close enough for target practice.

Justine's facial expression changed as tears rolled down her cheek bones. Murk blocked Justine's view of the blood bath that was about to take place.

Before Wet and Kelly-Boy could turn around, "Boom, boom!" the shots slammed into their chests and busted out of their backs. They hit the ground; lifeless.

Murk looked at Justine and said "Drive!"

Tears flowed down her face as she hit the accelerator and they pulled away.

CHAPTER 52 - ON THE SCENE

Dirty was driving along Sugar Creek Road when the call came in (911 Dispatch).

"We have a 911 emergency call from the Hidden Valley area. Two victims were shot and killed on Bilmark Street. We do not have any suspects."

"Copy, I'm on my way."

Damn Dirty thought. He was about to get off work and this shit had to happen. Why not let it happen on the next shift?

When he arrived at the scene, the ambulance was already there. Both bodies were lying on the ground with the white sheets covering them.

For certain, Dirty knew that was Kelly-Boy's car parked in the drive-way. Then as Dirty got out he said to himself, "Damn Kelly-Boy, what have you gotten yourself into now?"

Walking closer to the bodies Dirty asked the young officer, "What happened?"

"Looks like a drive-bye," the officer replied.

Dirty got down on one knee and grabbed a sheet and pulled it back. He looked at the young guy he never saw before that was Wet. As he moved to the next one, and pulled back the sheet, the other body was Kelly-Boy. Dead with his eyes wide open like he was in shock from what he had seen.

Dirty thought if he was even close to being fair, he could have saved two lives by taking them in for arrest. Now, they won't be coming back.

Dirty left the little bit of dope that was in the house so it would look like a drug-related crime. He thought that all blacks had in common was drugs and death.

Dirty pulled in his driveway, and sat for a moment just thinking what the fuck did dude know about him? Who else could've it been that killed Kelly-Boy? Either dude was a psychic or a professional killer. Maybe Pac-Man was right, it might have been the maintenance man who laid there in the middle of the parking lot.

But if the message dude was sending was supposed to scare Dirty, then he had his people fucked up. Dirty knows he's the law.

Once inside, before Dirty could get in the shower, his wife called him.

"Damn! We lost a helluva investment honey!" Sophelia said walking up to her husband to kiss him. "Regina ran off with a client."

"Don't worry about her. She'll be back, or I'll get another one who will be happy to take her place. I'm going to take a shower. Give me some sugar."

While in the shower, feeling the hot stream as the water splashed his body, Dirty couldn't figure out what happened. Could that have been the maintenance man that he shot and killed? Pac-Man was old, but far from being an old fool.

Dirty feared what he didn't know and the last thing he would let happen is someone harming his family.

He realized that the dude who was doing all the killing did him a favor. Fewer people in his business; fewer steps he had to take in order to get where he wanted to be.

Lying in the bed by himself, he looked up at the ceiling thinking to himself about where he went wrong, and if he regretted it ever happening.

Sophelia walked in the bedroom, more beautiful than ever; sweeter than cotton candy; soft like a marshmallow that would melt between your hands; a million dollar woman who would fuck the soul from your body. And to live without her, he would have to cash in every penny and start where he first began with nothing.

Sophelia was hot, wet and ready to fuck. Her movements were subtle. She leaned down and kissed Dirty's lips while slipping out of her satin panties. She worked her skillful tongue under her husband's neck as they moved together working up a body sweat as the temperature in the room escalated. She grabbed his dick and stuck it inside her pussy.

Dirty pumped hard like he was grudge fucking her, filling her every wall.

"Ahh...ahh...ahhh...aahh....ahh..Mmmmm...Daddy. You're hurting me, baby!"

Dirty didn't hear his wife because everything that was troubling him he took it out on her.

"Oh, God! I'm cumming honey!"

CHAPTER 53 - MURK

"I'm glad your father talked some sense into you when. I thought I was just about to be out of a job," Murk said looking like he was in one of his moods for sex.

Justine was so hurt inside that she could barely stand to look at Murk's face. And to think her father would take her life in the exchange for some drugs. Murk talked a good game, and the fact that he'd raped her, treated if she was some kinda nut rag was enough for her to try her own hands.

She was more lost mentally, after witnessing Pat-Rat's body laying there on the floor lifeless, bleeding to his death. The experience rapidly had taken its toll. "You are a cold-hearted-ass, nigga! Are you done, or you looking to kill again?" Justine asked.

"That was personal, they shot inside the house trying to kill you, and I can't understand, Justine, why you're so ungrateful. You are daddy's spoiled little girl."

"Bullshit! They did not shoot inside the house!" Justine said hysterically.

"Come here and give a hard working man some head."

"Don't you wish?"

"What happened with you catering to my needs?"

That's not part of the package deal; you think my father wouldn't tell me huh?"

"Why not?"

"You just might be out of a job, since you killed all your witnesses, stupid muthafucker!" Justine said looking in his eyes as Murk got up and approached her and grabbed her by the hair.

"Bitch! If you ever call me a muthafucker, it better be because I was getting off your mother! Do you understand me?"

"You're hurting me!"

"Huh? Do you understand, Bitch?"

"Yeah!"

"I'm going to get me something to eat, I would feed you, but you can't buy enough dicks behind the counter," Murk said laughing walking out the door.

Justine was thinking heavy, and couldn't yet come up with a solution. Then the thought hit her. She went in her pocket book and looked through a hundred numbers in Pat-Rat's phone looking for Dirty Cop.

She put the phone back up, and walked out the door as Murk was coming in at the same time. She bumped him, knocking herself against the wall.

"Don't stay out long, Baby, or I'll come for you."

Justine kept walking down the hall to the stairwell. She refused to wait for the elevator. Every step she took, she thought how far away she was from being where she wanted to be in life. And to think that her father would deceive her...

Walking through the Lobby of the Marriott Hotel, she went through the revolving doors, and smelled the fresh air and knew there was a God in heaven.

The sun was shining. She inhaled the air into her lungs and walked along W.T Harris.

Just 100 yards away, she saw the I-Hop. She was hungry, and walked at a fast pace with the breeze blowing in her face, feeling good and appreciative that life has more than what it appeared to offer, and it was a blessing that she was still living.

Once inside the door, the waitress asked how many.

Justine ensured the young lady she was by herself. She asked for a seat in the back as far away from the public as she could possibly be.

Justine ordered breakfast and looked through Pat-Rat's cell phone to connect with Dirty. She knew his name was there, but under what?

She didn't have any luck at all. What kept running through her mind was that she had been part of a murder spree and forced to be a part of something that will get her a long term prison sentence.

Justine was done, but she didn't want to go back to the hotel room. She needed a moment more before she would leave the restaurant and go back and deal with Murk.

* * *

WHAT

Dirty needed a bite to eat; he was taking his lunch break early. As he drove down W.T. Harris, he had several places to pick from. He saw the I-Hop and pulled in and parked.

The hostess sat him at a table. Dirty ordered a cup of coffee while looking at the paper and read about the maintenance man. In a way, it crushed Dirty that he was so unprofessional about the choices he had made. There was a picture of the victim who died for nothing along with a family portrait of his wife. He looked far away on the other side of the restaurant and spotted a young lady that looked like somebody he knew. Dirty studied her a minute until he realized it was Justine.

Dirty got up and told the waitress that he will be having breakfast over there at the far table with the young lady who was by herself.

Dirty was about to pull a chair out when Justine thought she saw a ghost.

"What's wrong? You look as if you've seen a ghost?" Dirty asked, serious enough to pull his gun to end her life.

"I was just trying to call you, believe it or not. That's why I was strolling through Rat's phone."

"So you can kill me, or to tell me you wanted some more of this dick?"

"Neither. I'm having problem with Murk. He's trying to take your life, and I've had enough watching innocent people die. Dirty, it may sound weird, but I need protection." Justine said with tears rolling from her eyes as if it no longer mattered if she lived or died.

"Even if I did believe you, I don't think I could trust you with everything that you know about me. Besides, who put the hit on me?" Dirty asked waiting on an answer and trying to figure it all out.

CHAPTER 54 - I-HOP

What kind of game is she trying to run?

After an hour of talking, Dirty figured that she was being trust worthy about the whole ordeal. Now Dirty knew why Pat-Rat was so cocky about everything he had done, because Justine was the go-to Bitch! And right now, she was so terrified because of the dope that Speedy had lost. This wasn't going to rest until he had it back or Dirty was dead.

Justine said her father had all the information he needed to do Dirty in. There were other options to save him, and that was give up the cheese for the product.

"So you're willing to set your boy up; I mean Murk?" Dirty asked?"

"Most definitely! But I need a place to secure mine without you coming back to kill me?"

Dirty knew Justine had enough on him to put him away for life, but she so-much wanted this chaos to be over that she was willing to keep her mouth shut. Dirty thought there wasn't any use in killing her because her father knew just as much as she did. Dirty was pretty much stuck in some shit that he had stepped in, and right now, he needed Justine alive and breathing because she most definitely was gonna be wanted by her family to comfort the matter instead of making it worst.

"You ain't got to worry about me killing you! I promise. I don't know how much my word means to you, but that's all I got."

"Why should I believe that, especially after you sent those guys back the second time? You had every intention of killing me!"

"I have to agree with you. Bit look at yourself; you're still alive. It just wasn't your time, Justine. I must admit, now that I've learned more about you just in this little time when I knew for a fact you could've been brought a nigga down sweetie," Dirty said with a meaningful look of concern.

"I need to have some insurance on your word, because your mouth can say anything. You fuck me, and then turn around, and are ready to kill me!"

***

"ONE-WAY"

Dirty let Justine leave after giving her the insurance that she was asking for.

Walking down the street heading toward the hotel she spotted the rental car that Murk was driving. Justine hadn't realized her phone was off. She turned it back on and it beeped 4 times.

Murk spotted her walking down the opposite direction from where he was coming from. He was ready to beat her ass. She kept walking when finally they came together.

"Where the fuck have you been, trick?" Murk asked as he grabbed her shirt and pulled her along.

Dirty pulled up behind them, blinking his lights and blowing his horn. Murk turned around and was caught off guard when Dirty jumped out and pointed his gun at him while telling Murk to get on the ground.

Murk, not realizing who Dirty was, did as he was told.

Murk was on both knees with his hands behind his head when Dirty grabbed him and smashed his face in the concrete.

"Ma'am?" Dirty asked, "Are you alright?"

"Yeah! He didn't do anything, officer. Please let him go!"

"See there, Officer? Be a nice boy and release me," Murk said laughing with his lips bleeding.

I'll have to ask you to please step back, ma'am," Dirty said as he searched Murk. He didn't have a weapon or I.D on him.

"Where is your I.D., sir?"

"You heard the lady, I haven't done nothing officer."

"I'll need to take him down town to I.D him unless you can provide me with some form of identification."

"Justine! Justine, go to our room and get my I.D, It's on the coffee table," Murk told her as he lay on the ground.

"I'll be back," Justine replied

Dirty now roughed Murk into the backseat of the police car, closing the door behind him. Dirty got in, took his hat off, and turned around so Murk was able to see his face.

"The dirty cop! Did Justine tell you where I was at? C'mon cop, it's alright. You can snitch on her. Ain't that what y'all do best?" Murk asked laughing.

"Damn sure is," Dirty said as he pulled off looking crazy.

Murk realized that they had passed the hotel. "Officer? Hey? Umm, Pig, where are we going?"

"I'm taking you to jail for murders that you committed in the Hidden Valley area. Anymore questions?"

"Yeah!"

"What?"

"Where's your witness? Huh? Hello, Pig?"

"Damn! You're right. You killed them all. I can't prove it. Fuck! What was I thinking? I got a better place for you where you will never have to worry about killing anyone else."

"Yeah! But you were next," Murk said laughing at Dirty.

"You can't threaten an officer of the law, son. Where are you from?"

"I would say your mommy then we wouldn't be going through what we are going through with this little altercation, because we would be brothers."

"You got mommy jokes, huh? Yeah... Well my mother is dead," Murk replied trying to figure where this was going.

"Ummm... Damn sad because my mom got killed too. Damn! We could be brothers. I did come from your mommy," Murk said laughing.

Dirty was on the Highway 85 heading north but trying to get onto South 85. They both rode in silence.

Dirty believed him about his mother being murdered-because Dirty had a brother who was given up for adoption before he was born. Whatever the situation, it didn't matter, because Dirty had plans for Murk.

CHAPTER 55 - "THE RIDE"

"Hey, let's make a deal," Murk said.

"You ain't in no position to be making any deals," Dirty told Murk.

"C'mon, Cop! Don't be so diplomatic. We're both arrogant as hell. Let's make a deal. Give the dope back and we all go home to our loved ones and nobody gets killed."

"That's not a deal, it sounds as if you're giving me no alternatives, Killer," Dirty said looking in the review mirror at him smiling.

"It's not Killer, it's Murk!"

"Well they both mean the same thing."

"What about the proposition I just offered?"

"Let's just say that I keep the dope and my life, and just get rid of yours."

"That wouldn't be smart at all, because Justine knows that we're together, and trust me, when she tells her father, he'll send some more goons.

"What was he thinking sending you?"

"This accident I was caught on some technicality, that's all."

Dirty couldn't believe that Murk went into a laugh as if he was losing his mind, then laughed and dropped a few tears from his face. Dirty thought how this wasn't normal. Dirty looked for a reason to let him live, but just couldn't find one. Dirty even thought how they had some similarities, but his life was at stake along with his family. Better Murk, than him.

Pulling into the wooded area, they drove down a dead end road where no one could even guess about their location. Dirty got out of the car and opened the trunk, grabbing a 40 caliber, and placed it in the back of his belt of his uniform. He opened the back door as Murk drug one leg out.

Never in a million years did Murk ever think that he would leave this world like this. He felt a cold chill that circulated his body in the worst way. And he knew killers didn't go out crying.

"Get on your knees. A pig – is that what you called me?" Dirty asked.

"Not me, I think it was more a hog with big nuts who eats everything that he put his face in."

"Murk, I like you. You're an ambitious kind of guy."

"Shit. You can't like me. You're about to kill me. How ambitious is that?"

"Open your mouth," Dirty said looking straight in Murk eyes.

"I'm not opening my mouth for you to stick the barrel in it, Pig."

Boom, Boom! And one more to his chest.

"I bet you won't come back from this one."

* * *

HOTEL

Justine waited patiently for Murk to call from the county jail so she could go pick him up. Murk was her responsibility and still she hadn't heard a word from him.

She had Dirty's cell number and thought that she would call him.

"Hello," Dirty said.

"What's up? I mean, what's going on?"

"You ain't going to believe this shit! Get your shit together and I'll pick you up," Dirty said.

"Oh God! What happened?" Justine asked rushing herself to get her things.

She left the hotel and walked back up the street to the I-Hop restaurant.

She called Dirty on the way and said, "I'm at the I-Hop."

Ten minutes went by while Justine sat at a table. She watched every human-being who walked in and out the door, but no sign of Dirty.

The waitress asked if she wanted to order and again she said no.

Right now it was difficult for her to swallow her own spit. Justine knew that it was her first instinct that she needed to trust, and right now it was with a Dirty Cop.

CHAPTER 56 - I-HOP

Dirty finally came through the door of the restaurant, and looked directly at Justine. She was unsure about the move, and most definitely didn't want to die.

Dirty took a seat.

"What happened?" Justine asked terrified.

"Settle down! There's no telling where he's at! Let's go."

Justine, not thinking, followed Dirty to the car. He opened the door for her on the passenger side, and then he got in. Before leaving the parking lot, Dirty asked her a few questions.

"Can your father be trusted?"

"No! Not right now. If he found out anything about me trying to help you, oh man…"

"Okay, I'm thinking."

"What am I going to do? Where will I stay?"

"Don't worry! I've got a place for you and it's safe until we can figure out what's up with the dude's next move, ummm… Murk, is that right?"

Dirty pulled out of the I-Hop parking lot and listened to Justine about confiding with the enemy. She was against her father. Surely he would disown her as a daughter. Dirty made a few calls and got the answer he was looking for.

Outside the Penthouse, Dirty called CeCe. She came out the front door and Dirty excused himself to go to her.

"I need for you let her stay in Regina's room."

"Why?"

"It's a long story, but I can assure you that once she get's comfortable with herself she'll most definitely want to get paid, especially with your help."

"Dirty's got so many tricks; I can't do nothing but ride out with a nigga! Who is she?"

"Justine! Let's just get her inside and comfortable, I know she's probably tired."

Dirty went back to the cruiser and brought Justine in the house. He turned around and left.

What Dirty got from Justine is her father knew people in places, like his Chief of Police. Everybody that knew something was now in a place Dirty didn't have to worry about. It's late and it wouldn't be long before Dirty was off work. Dirty knew business had been good for the most part, because Kingston had been pushing the dope like a pro.

Pulling in at home Dirty saw the light on the little office where Sophelia spent 75% of her time. Dirty knew that he loved his wife and could not fault his wife when he was more wrong then her.

Dirty went inside and there at the computer, she was reading a message from her e-mail from her L.T., who was stationed in Fort Bragg. The message stated: I'm sorry things didn't work out, but with your help I still came up on top with one of your escort service clients. I have to beat her at times, but I will make her a damn good wife. That's what I do. At ease, Soldier.

Dirty stood over his wife's shoulder, and said. "How did he know about the escort service?"

"Apparently from the guys, because I didn't tell him, Honey!"

"Don't worry about it. I've got plans for him, and to get her back."

"He's beating her," Sophelia said, concerned for Regina's life.

"Yeah! If he only knew how I felt about a man putting his hands on a woman!"

"What are you suggesting?"

"Call his cell phone, and set up a date!"

"You sure, Honey?"

"Yeah baby! No more using the computer."

Dirty said to himself walking away going down to his basement, "Why would CeCe and Monica lie about the reason she left the house?"

Opening the safe, Dirty picked though the money, and was staggered with his accomplishment, and proud of himself in the length of time he did it. But there was more to be made. But some of the money felt different from the others. But right now, he wasn't concerned about that.

CHAPTER 57 - NEXT MORNING

Dirty kissed his wife before he left for work. Pulling out of the drive-way, his phone rang. He looked at his caller I.D. and saw that it was Kingston. Right away Dirty answered the phone. "Hello," Dirty said.

"What's up?" Kingston asked.

"You tell me."

"You tell me?"

"I got big business for you, Dirty! That's if you got it?"

"I guess it depends on what you're spending?"

"One of my fans I've been dealing with for many years is trying to get 20 of them things."

Dirty thought how the deal by itself sounded good but right now Dirty was focused on something more important and something that he had being waiting to do for a long time.

"Maybe tomorrow I'll meet your man," Dirty said.

"You don't have to meet him, everything I do is professional, just me, and you!"

"I'll be there to see the money!"

"And you can take it with you."

"Yeah!"

Dirty went to the precinct and fixed a cup of hot coffee. Before returning to his desk, the Chief pointed and told Dirty to come in his office.

"Have a seat, I'll be right back," the Chief of Police said walking out the door.

Dirty's mind raced as he looked out of the blinds of the office. There were other officers looking in as if they were fishing, and yet knew what the fuck was going on, because Dirty damn sure didn't.

Still looking out, Dirty saw that the Chief was shaking the hand of a man who had on a two-piece suit and looked as if he could be a Fed.

But Dirty knew now wasn't the time to be sweating because now they were walking together toward the office.

"Carlos," said the man in the two-piece suit.

"Yes Sir! How can I help you?" Dirty said trying like hell not to act any different than he usually does around the Chief.

They were sitting in their chairs while the young man in the suit fumbled through a big envelop that apparently had some photos in it.

"My name is Agent Massy. I'm with the Federal Government. Before you answer these questions, do you know your rights?"

"Yeah....I'm pretty much familiar with them," Dirty replied giving the young man his full attention.

They both laughed, but Dirty didn't feel real healthy with the sarcasm.

Now Carlos was looking at some unfamiliar faces in the photos when he came across one of J.J. laying there on the ground face down. Whatever tactics the agent was trying, it would have possibly worked if Dirty would've looked at the pictures a few more minutes after seeing his best friend laying there dead. Quickly, Dirty took a glimpse at his Chief and the possibility that he knew a whole lot more than he'd pretended.

"I heard J.J. was a good friend of yours? Here, take look at his pictures. Surely you miss him, don't you?" the agent asked.

"Yeah, I miss him because he was more than just a friend. He was like a counselor for me to confide in."

"A friend like that doesn't come along every day, Mr. Bowmen; I bet you really miss him, huh?"

"Cut the games! What's going on?" Dirty asked, demanding some answers. He felt like the dude was trying to play him.

"Well, if you insist. We have a report here, filed by a young man. It's a report on ummm... let me see... Carlos. Bowmen, that is you, right?"

"Yeah!" he said, frustrated, remembering not to get beside himself.

"He claims you extorted him, then he came up dead, after officer J.J. was killed. I don't want to get ahead of myself. Ummm.... Chief, J.J. was assigned to this case after the young man filed on Mr. Bowmen right?"

"Yes, sir," the Chief replied.

Damn, Dirty thought, this little jar-head son-of-bitch was trying to put Dirty behind bars. What caught Dirty's attention was not just what Justine said, but what the Chief implemented about the gun being found inside of Pat-Rat's house which was obviously an attempt to frame a murder weapon on a guy that was dead.

After about three hours, Dirty hung in there tight when he felt the Chief question him even more than the agent did. Dirty secured his ground that he stood on especially with the charges they made assumptions about.

But Dirty thought how they ran off the road of the path that could've truly accused him of his wrong doing.

"Okay Mr. Bowmen, you can leave. If we need to talk again, we know where to find you.

CHAPTER 58

Dirty left the parking lot of the police precinct and couldn't believe how close he was to being a suspect of a Capital Murder and how the federal agent assured him that it was more involved in this matter. He felt a sharp pain in his gut, since he expected it would be over by now.

Out of all this, Justine is what bothered him the most. She could end his career. He thought if she was going to talk, she would have done that the first time when he wanted to kill her.

Dirty called his wife to see what the business was as far as him wanting to meet with the Lieutenant

The phone rang several times; finally, he heard his wife's voice, "Hello?" she said as she stretched and rolled her hot body over in bed to gain better position.

"Baby! What's up?" Dirty asked.

"What do you mean?" she asked.

"You know, with the Lieutenant?"

"Honey, I'm supposed to call him around 6 o'clock this afternoon. Did you forget?"

Yeah, yeah! That's right, ummm....damn! What was I going to tell you? Yeah. Umm...do you have a security code for the escort service?"

"Yeah! Why?"

"It's nothing that you're doing; it's my job. They're cracking down on the case with J.J., that's all.

"You told me that they solved that case, remember?"

"Yeah, I know! Well look, call me later and don't let me slip on the time."

"Honey, are you sure you're alright?"

"I'm fine... I'm thinking about coming home and making love to my wife."

"You know that's impossible, your son will be here any minute."

"Give him my love, sweetie."

Dirty wanted to go by and talk with Justine when he had her thinking that her life was in danger. She wouldn't answer her phone. He figured if he needed to talk with her Dirty would call the Penthouse number. "Wild" he thought of how his mind raced in many directions. Surely Dirty has the instinct to push aside something to overthrow the law, but being a part of it, triggered his mentality that his fun and games now were more serious than he could ever anticipate.

(911)

"We have an emergency call in the Hidden Valley area. There's been a report on some shooting on Cinderella and Candy Stick St."

"Copy! I'm on my way!"

Dirty hurried to get to the location. And when he arrived, there in the middle of the street was a little kid, couldn't have been more than 5 years old with his mother going hysterical, out of her mind.

"Please get back!" Dirty said feeling the little boy for a pulse.

The little boy was caught up in a shoot out. They left him bleeding from his side. Dirty pumped the little boy's chest until the ambulance showed up. They were able to keep the little man breathing.

Dirty asked some questions from the people that were close and didn't bother to want to help because they were scared for their own lives.

After about a few hours, Dirty decided to leave the neighborhood head closer to home.

* * *

PENTHOUSE

CeCe walked one of the clients that she had just fucked to the front door as Justine sat comfortably in the living room watching T.V. alone. CeCe sat down beside her, and said, "Dude put a fucking on me! One more like that and I'm done!" she said leaning back on the couch.

"If that dick is like that, shit I need one like that, girl" Justine replied.

"Shit! At least get paid for it!"

"I don't know!"

"What? C'mon girl! We always can get dick for free, at least let'em pay you for it."

Justine thought if she was going to sit in the Penthouse 24-7. Why not get her fuck on?

After CeCe convinced her, not wasting anytime she called Sophelia, and got Justine on the hook-up. CeCe agreed to fix her hair. CeCe and Justine were on the way down the hall-way when Monica came out of her room with her client.

"I'm not going to ask you how you got hooked up with Dirty?"

"Good! Because it's a long story, and if I explain it to you, regardless how it may sound, you probably would think I was telling a story."

"Girl, he's the dirtiest cop here in the Queen City. Even N.Y.P.D in my hometown couldn't touch this muthafucker.

Justine listened to CeCe as she kept on about Dirty. There wasn't anything she had said that she didn't know.

"Girl, that was Sophelia and she got you a hook-up already. Just think, while you are here stack your money so you will be straight, so you can do as you please when you leave," CeCe whispered as she stared at Justine.

"Oh God! You look beautiful, Justine!" CeCe said pumping her ego to do something she really didn't know if she had the guts to do.

"Get up! Let me see them butt cheeks," CeCe said as she finished with her hair. "Make sure you have condoms."

"No I don't," Justine busted out and said.

"I'll get her some. I'll be back!" Monica said as she walked out of the bedroom.

"Make sure dude's doesn't punch a hole in their rubbers. They're good for that!" CeCe warned her.

CeCe left the bedroom too leaving Justine alone to get her thoughts together. Justine knew that she was overdue for a good fucking. She remembered CeCe rehearsing over and over again about the dick that had her in a zone.

Then she heard a knock at the door, when Justine said, "Yeah."

"Can I come in, please?" Monica yelled.

"Yeah, what's up?"

"Sometimes we get lucky, and some get luckier than the rest, but your first client is here!"

"Are you serious?" she asked all excited and eager to see who the stranger was that she had to fuck.

"You ready?" Monica asked looking sad.

"What does he look like?"

"I'll tell you like a friend once told me—it's not what they look like, it's business!"

Monica and Justine walked out of the bedroom and up the hall. There in the living room stood Big Flex who made Justine looked like an ant eater.

CHAPTER 59

Dirty sat inside his patrol car parked where he and J.J. used to meet. Dirty felt he would've killed his own father if he took away the food he had worked so hard to get.

He was waiting patiently for the phone call he was expecting from his wife; so far nothing. He listened to Power 97.9, relaxing with some heavy thoughts.

Time passed. Dirty couldn't wait any longer. He decided to call his wife. The phone rang six times before Sophelia picked up.

"Hello!" she said as if she was out of breath.

"Damn! Are you alright?" Dirty asked.

"Yeah..." she said laughing, "Stop! You better stop! I'm playing with little Carlos, Jr."

"What is he doing?"

"Stop! He's kicking me," she said joyfully playing.

"Tell him that Daddy loves him."

"Hold on, you want to talk with him?"

"Put him on the phone."

"Daddy!! Mommy's hitting me, that's why I'm hitting her."

"That's my son, if anyone put their hands on you, make sure you hit them back."

After Dirty was done talking with little Carlos, Sophelia told her husband everything was lined up.

Carlos didn't have the slightest idea what they really talked about. She did cheat on him, so what else could she possibly do to hurt him again? She did worse things in life than spread her legs for a man giving him what she said she'd never do for another; till death do us part.

After hanging up, Dirty sat in his car. No longer listening to the radio, he was zoned out. Behind it all, on the other side of the coin was the reality and principles that were important to people in their daily lives. And that was something Dirty chose to be a part of—to protect and serve.

Dirty drove off and decided he wanted to ride by the Penthouse when he knew that Justine at the moment needed to be his friend because he couldn't stop thinking how the Chief of Police was directing the agent to some points that the agent didn't bother to look at.

Pulling in the driveway Dirty saw no sign of any vehicles, nor did he see Monica's car anywhere. Knocking on the door, he heard a voice that might have sounded like CeCe's. She came to the door with a see-through night grown on. She said, "Come in Dirty!"

"What's up?" Dirty asked looking at CeCe's body.

"Don't even try it! We've tried that before, remember?" she said walking off going to the back.

Dirty sat down in the living room and could remember when there was only the carpet and couch, but now the Penthouse was so compact and looked different. The women had really put some work into the place. CeCe came back up the hall, now dressed in some jeans.

"Dirty, who you looking for?"

"Where is Justine?"

"They left to go pick up some food."

'Have you seen Regina? Has she come back or at least tried to pick up her check?" Dirty asked looking at CeCe to see if she showed any signs lying.

"Ummmm...No she hasn't. I'm surprised especially when the money belonged to her. And she's smoking."

"Damn, did it ever appear that she could be hurt? I mean, she was a friend regardless if she smokes or not." Dirty said with his head down.

"Yeah! I don't know. Ask Monica."

Dirty's phone rang. The caller ID showed it was Sophelia! Then he put his finger to his lips telling CeCe to hold on, and then answered the phone just as Justine and Monica were walking through the door and called Dirty's name.

"Where are you, Honey?" Sophelia asked.

"I'm about to walk out of the office. Can I call you back, please? It will only take a few minutes." Click!

"Damn, this officer of the law, dirty than the niggas on the streets trying to get a dollar," Monica said.

Quickly Dirty thought if this bitch didn't hush her damn mouth he would frame her ass with her own gun and leave her ass to rot in jail.

Dirty asked to speak with Justine in private.

They walked in the back to her room and closed the door behind them. Dirty sat down on the bed and watched Justine with her jeans that fit perfectly on her little round ass.

"Justine, have you heard anything?"

"How? I was told not to use my own phone!"

"Yeah that's right, umm...I've been patrolling the streets looking for any sign of him," Dirty said lying as if she didn't know that Dirty had some shit with him.

"I've got to make a run. If you need me, call! You still got my number, right?"

"Yeah!"

Dirty said his goodbyes to the girls and left. Once outside, he quickly dialed his wife.

CHAPTER 60 - MEAN WHILE

"Where are you, Dirty?" Sophelia asked with a lot of animosity as if she knew her husband was playing games.

"I'm in my car. "

"What's so good about wanting to hurt someone Carlos?"

"Look Baby! I don't have the slightest idea what's running through your little mind, but I haven't done anything to hurt you. I just want to put this nigga in check. Now if you feeling something else, then you need to move your shit and go live with that lame azz."

Click, he hung up.

Dirty knew he couldn't get over this but Sophelia was making shit difficult because Dirty refused to forget.

Driving towards home, Dirty's cell phone started ringing and this time it was Kingston. He had almost forgotten about the dude.

"What's up, Kingston?"

"You know what's up. My people are trying to set up a meeting with you," Kingston replied sounding like he was frustrated.

"Let's set this up for tomorrow when I can take the day off; is that cool?"

"Yeah, Man!"

Dirty thought if Kingston knew the deal, he wouldn't rush things because Dirty thought this lick would most definitely set him and his family straight.

Pulling in his drive-way, Dirty sat in the car for a minute before he went inside. He wanted to get his head together so he wouldn't mess around and said something that later on that he would regret.

"Dirty I'm going to ask you again—where have you have been? Do you actually think you have a relationship with them girls like I have! Huh?"

"Look Honey! I'm sorry. It's just that I needed to talk to Justine."

"Haven't you fucked her, too?"

"Nah, far from it. There's just so much shit going on with my job. She's in witness protection."

Sophelia was far from stupid. If that was the game he wanted to play, then fine. She knew the city police would never handle witness protection."

They stared at each other like they were trying to learn each other all over again. One thing for sure, Dirty loved his wife and she loved him.

"There's being a change of plans with the L.T."

"What do you mean?"

"He's decided to send Regina back on the bus."

Dirty didn't like what he heard because they had put in some time talking about this for this cocky son-of-bitch to back out at the last minute. But what more could Dirty do? Go to the army base? That was something he wanted to do but now, he was frustrated to the point of driving around the neighborhood.

Fuck work. Every time Dirty thought about Lieutenant Brown sticking his dick in his wife and then taking and beating one of his bitches from the crib, Dirty got madder. Sophelia thinks she's smoothed the situation. Maybe this was the kind of punishment Sophelia was used to, or needed Dirty thought to himself.

Dirty parked in front of his garage and called his Chief to explain that he had an emergency at home so the Chief needed to have someone replace him.

Walking in the house, Dirty saw Sophelia sitting on the couch smoking a cigarette. Smoking was not allowed in the house, yet there she was.

Sophelia thought Dirty must know something was missing from the picture, but she couldn't tell for sure.

Dirty had a seat beside her and put his hand on her thighs, stopping Sophelia from getting up.

"Wait! Please hear me out, Baby."

"What? What are you talking about, Carlos?"

"Damn how can I put this, hmm…. Damn. I'm under investigation at work."

"For what? J.J.?"

Dirty never said a word.

"Did you kill J.J., Carlos? Please don't lie to me!"

"No! I didn't. But just because I didn't pull the trigger doesn't mean I'm not a killer. And it doesn't stop me from wanting to kill your L.T!"

"Please Carlos let's just move on with our lives baby. Let's move and leave all of this behind us. I thought I knew you. When I look in your eyes, you're a complete stranger; that's so hard for me to accept. If you can't be trusted now, don't give me an answer that's going to be a lie because I can't take it anymore," Sophelia said as she grabbed Carlos by his face.

Carlos' eyes were a glare like there was something that he really wanted to say. "If that's the way you really feel, I will not lie. After I go see this guy and drop off the rest of these drugs, we can move on some place far away."

"Drugs?"

Dirty put a finger up to her lips and whispered loud enough for her to hear. "This is it! I promise you. I've got some business to handle and then we're outta here."

CHAPTER 61 - HOME

Dirty took a hot shower. As the water splashed over his body he thought about the last robbery he was gonna do.

While changing clothes, he called Kingston's cell phone.

"Yo, what kinda games are you into, Dirty? I got people on hold when they thinking a nigga playing games with them," Kingston said.

"Chill out! I'm on my way, but it ain't gonna be to conduct business yet."

"Shit. I told you from the beginning you didn't have to meet them," Kingston said about fed up with Dirty's bullshit.

After hanging up, Dirty put his gun in his back, hiding it under his shirt. He opened the door to his truck, got in and left, heading to Kingston's crib.

Dirty turned the music down as he turned onto Timmerbrook where Kingston sold his drugs. At the end of the street, Dirty parked his car looking around to see if he recognized any unwanted guest or vehicles.

The night was surrounded with street lights with little limited traffic. Normally, Timmerbrook was lit up like Broadway.

Dirty called Kingston's phone. .

"Yeah! Where are you at?" Kingston asked answering on the second ring.

"I'm at the door."

"You don't have any drugs in the house, do you?"

"What! This is a drug house dude." Click, Kingston hung up.

Dirty thought how he might have to check Kingston with his bitch-ass attitude. Still standing on the porch, he walked to the front door and carefully looked around before pushing the door wide open to go in.

Kingston came around the corner and said, "Come on in the kitchen, he's not here yet!"

Once inside, Dirty thought it didn't look like a spot for a crack house. He went in the kitchen and saw a small table and refrigerator, very clean and appropriate; he felt comfortable.

Then Kingston asked, "You want something to drink?"

"Nah! What about a blunt?"

"Damn!!!! You are just a straight gangsta-ass cop. What gives you the motivation to do the shit you be doing?" Kingston asked.

Dirty went into a deep thought and carefully trying to read what the fuck Kingston just said. 'The shit you be doing' caught Dirty's undivided attention.

"What do you mean?" Dirty asked.

"Your badges! Give y'all authority to run the fucking world and get away with it."

"Don't be mistaken. I do my job and protect and serve."

***

Kingston opened a half gallon of Hennessy and they drank and talked shit to one another, shot after a shot.

"Dirty! How long you been a cop?"

"Six years, why? Why are you asking me so many damn questions? You need my badges, muthafucker??!"

"Nigga, I'm far from being a damn snitch! You can't extort me, nigga!"

"What? Where did you get that? Besides, where are your people? I'm about to leave."

Dirty figured Kingston knew a lot more than he acted.

'What's wrong? Chill... They'll be here in a minute or two."

"They? I thought we agreed not to meet but one," Dirty said looking confused.

"Nah, cop! That's something you agreed to."

"I'm out," Dirty said as he got up to leave. He was about to turn his back on Kingston, when Dirty ran into a couple handguns.

The two men that were holding the guns on Dirty were straight killers. When this other man walked between the gunmen and called Dirty out by his real name.

"Carlos, hold on son. First of all, let me pat you down to make sure I'm safe."

The man searched Dirty and found his handgun under his belt behind him. He put the gun inside his pocket.

Dirty realized that he had been set-up because he'd never told anyone his real name. All of this was starting to make sense. The Federal agent asking questions about J.J. But where did Kingston fit in? Dirty kept thinking. Kingston had made it perfectly clear he fit in where the Big Boy's played.

"Now son, please hear me out. But first, go ahead and have a seat. I'm going to talk and you just answer me. That's all I want you to do. Go ahead and get comfortable."

Dirty did exactly what he was told.

Kingston walked off leaving Dirty with the other three men in the kitchen. He had sweat on his forehead. Dirty couldn't understand what was talking place, especially when he wasn't traveling with anything. What could these niggas want?

Then Kingston returned back to the kitchen carrying 5 of the fifteen kilos of cocaine that Dirty had given him.

CHAPTER 62 - PENTHOUSE

Cece heard two knocks at the door. When she opened it, there on the front porch stood Regina with her bags. CeCe invited Regina in.

Once she was inside, Regina stood in the light. She had a black eye and it looked as if she had been abused and used.

"Damn, girl! What's happened to you? What the fuck?" CeCe yelled out.

"Who done it?" Monica asked while Justine ran in the living room after hearing the commotion.

Justine stopped in her tracks and when she saw Regina for the first time. From what she had heard about Regina previously, Justine thought how pretty she was.

"Girl, that nigga is crazy! When I thought I had a good man, he actually put my head in the commode and when I tried to come up for air, he flushed the toilet and said breathe while you can before it fills back up. I thought I was going to die!" Regina said looking like she needed a friend.

"Next time, you better think before running off with G.I. Joe's, them muthafuckers are crazy! Since it's in the air, I'll tell you what mine tried to do. He sent me out of the room—he wanted to play hide and seek. Girl, I said what the fuck," Monica said with her arm in the air. "Hold on, let me finish telling you. Now, there's only a big-ass closet and the bed, nothing much to chase from to dusky yourself, right! Check this shit out—I'm ass-naked when I come back in the room. I figured I would look out the window. Where else could he have been? Girls! This muthafucker was in the attic!"

They all laughed.

"The nigga wanted his money worth."

Sitting in the living room, all of them together tried to come up with a solution. Regina agreed to stay and try to work herself back in the groove.

CeCe decided she would call Sophelia in the morning,

It was pretty late and they all went to their bedrooms. Regina said she would sleep in the living room.

Regina made herself comfortable and looking up at the ceiling, she wondered how Dirty would take her running out on him. She really didn't know if he would accept that. She tried her hardest to get comfortable but it was impossible, because she was worried about her health. She cried and knew this wasn't the place she needed to be. She grabbed her bag and left the Penthouse.

HOSPITAL 2:30 IN THE MORNING

Sophelia rushed through the double doors of the hospital and asked the nurse which room was Regina Coats in.

She got on the elevator and thought what have I done? Sophelia felt like she was to blame for this all.

The elevator stopped and Sophelia stepped off. She stood at Regina's door trying to stop the tears before going into the room.

She saw Regina lying on her side in a knot, completely zoned-out. Sophelia pulled up a chair and stroked Regina's hair. She didn't want to ask how she felt. Just the thought of what Regina had described when leaving the Penthouse just an hour ago was enough to make Sophelia want to take her gun and blow the son-of-bitch's brain out his head.

There were a knock on the door.

Sophelia said, "Come in!"

It was a policewoman and a young lady from Social Service.

"I have some questions that I need to ask you. Is that alright?" the young lady from Social Services said to Regina.

"Yeah!" she replied.

As Sophelia tried to get up, Regina grabbed her hand. She didn't want her to leave. Sophelia looked at the young lady.

"It's okay! You can stay if that's going to make her comfortable so that we are able to put this guy behind bars."

"Okay, Regina. I'll stay. I'm not going anywhere, I promise. I'll stay right here, okay," Sophelia said trying to comfort Regina who had tears falling from her eyes. Sophelia didn't, or couldn't, imagine what she was going through.

Sophelia mind raced at first because she knew the escort service could get her some prison time if Regina said the wrong things.

The young girl from Social Service took the chair directly in front of Regina with her pen and forms with the policewoman close enough to hear everything.

"Can I see, please? Can we pull up your gown just enough so we can witness the scar?" the young social worker asked.

Sophelia had a perfect view of where L.T Brown stuck a broom stick up her pussy and corrupted her insides. Regina had no choice but to have surgery.

CHAPTER 63 - SITUATION

Dirty couldn't believe his eyes seeing all 15 kilos Kingston brought and sat there in his face. They had the same seal as the packages he had once given. Dirty had been fooled. He thought Kingston was a street drug dealer and now, they had piled some serious weight on him.

The middle-aged man with gray hair who had told Dirty to have a seat spoke, "Son! You see those packages? Yeah, them right there belongs to me?" Speedy said with a look that meant business.

"Well, if they're yours, you can have them," Dirty replied.

"Where's are the rest of them, huh?"

"That's it! There are no more."

"You got games? You want to play I see."

Bump, bump, bump, upside Dirty's head with some brass knuckles. "You want some? C'mon! Your hands aren't tied. Get the fuck up," Speedy demanded.

Dirty wasn't a fool. What were his chances running past this old man and getting past the other two with the guns? Apparently for this guy to want to fight, Dirty thought he must know something.

So Dirty knew that he would pass on the challenge. "Hey, Kingston! Talk to your friend. I'll be back."

Giving them a few minutes, they walked out the kitchen and Kingston had a seat right in front of Dirty.

"Yo man! You're making things difficult. I'm going to be straight with you. The dope you got is Speedy's. Hopefully, you haven't killed his daughter because she ain't anywhere to be found. It's possible that you killed Murk, but he doesn't care about that. It's his daughter and dope he's here for. I've been dealing with Pat-Rat for a minute. You're right, it's been dry prior to the packages you brought me. That's why I asked you about the seal on the dope because I knew it was Speedy's. I was for sure, but I had to make sure," Kingston said trying to be slick.

"I ain't got shit! I don't know anything about Murk or his daughter," Dirty replied being sincere trying to protect the dope money and drugs.

"Damn! Don't be stupid. The man knows you a cop. Dirty, he knows where you live. Shit!!!! He knows everything. He's not to be fucked with, don't you understand?"

"What happens if I just get up and walk out?"

"Well, if you do, your ass is as good as shot! You got caught up in the game. Don't lose your life man. I don't know what else to tell you." Kingston said looking like he was for real about the whole ordeal.

As they sat in silence, Dirty's heart pounded as he tried to figure a way out. Suddenly, he realized that this was a grown man's game and some get beat at their own game.

Dirty's cell phone was in the truck and if he didn't answer his phone, his wife would be very concerned. Surely the dope he had wasn't worth losing his family. Who's to say if the dude gets his drugs that Dirty would still live?

Just then, they walk back in the room. "What's it going to be, son?" Speedy said calmly waiting for a reply from the dirty cop.

"Yeah! I got you," Dirty said.

"What about my daughter, did you kill her?"

"Nah! She's safe."

"How do you expect me to believe you?"

"You want to talk to her?"

"Can I?" Speedy asked as if everything he had doubted was now a reality from a bad dream.

Kingston grabbed the house phone and handed it to Dirty.

Blocking the number, Dirty dialed the Penthouse. For a moment, no one answer it. Then he heard, "Hello!"

"Who is this?" Dirty asked."

"Justine!"

"Justine, this is Dirty!"

"Where have you 'been? Everybody's been calling you. Your wife is at the hospital."

"What's wrong with Sophelia?" Dirty asked thinking to himself if this muthafucker had hurt her...

"No! It's Regina," Justine said.

Dirty felt a little relief and asked, "Which hospital?"

"Carolina Medical!"

"Somebody wants to talk to you."

"Who?"

"Justine! Justine is that you?"

"Daddy!"

"Yeah baby! Are you alright?"

"Why wouldn't I be?"

Dirty jumped up and headed out of the kitchen when the two men blocked his path.

Speedy turned around and said "I expect for you to do the right thing and not spend all the money you made from the kilos we purchased from you! It's not real. It's counterfeit," Speedy said holding the phone tight in his hand.

***

HOSPITAL

Arriving at the hospital, Dirty had the thrill of still being alive, he knew his wife would never steer him in the wrong direction.

When he got off on the 5th floor where Regina was, there in the hall stood Sophelia, CeCe, and Monica sharing a moment of disbelief for their girlfriend. Despite the difficulties she may have had in her past, they loved Regina.

Sophelia saw Dirty and ran up and hugged him. "Honey! You're not going to believe what happened to Regina?"

"What's going on?" Dirty asked looking at the other girls with dried tears that ran down their cheeks.

They all sat down and got a better understanding of what was going on. But before anyone of them lost their sanity and wanted to do something to react off impulse, Sophelia insured everybody that he would get a dishonorable discharge and a long prison term for his actions. Sophelia suggested that they let the law do their jobs.

When Dirty thought about the shit he been through and almost losing his life, he decided to let the law take care of it.

Dirty left the women at the hospital and decided to keep his end of the bargain with Speedy. One thing for sure, he wasn't going to forget the blows he received upside of his head. He knew there was a difference—beating the shit out of a person and then taking his shit and let'em live.

Dirty realized there was something about the money he once felt.

Dirty packed the rest of the dope inside the back of his S.U.V. and then he called Kingston.

"Yeah! What's up, Dirty?"

"Where you want to meet?" Dirty asked.

"You tell me; you're the law."

"Let's meet at the car wash on North Tryon Street."

"Hey, Dirty?"

"Yeah!"

"I'm glad you decided to do the right thing. Speedy already had a stakeout to kill you and your family."

"How did Speedy find out about my family, Kingston?" Dirty asked not sure that Kingston would tell him anything. His curiosity was running wild from what he had already gathered from Justine.

"Yo, Dirty. This is a lot bigger than you and me. Together, we're both peons. What if I told you that I wouldn't be able to sell drugs nowhere on the streets of Charlotte. Everything is tied up in an organization that's surrounded in your Justine's apartment.

My money and yours together couldn't buy a share of the profit; you just hit the wrong stash Dirty. Hey, did you honestly think I would introduce you to the connect?"

"Shit! I don't know what to believe anymore, but yeah!"

"C'mon man!!!! You're a Cop."

Dirty kept the promise and dropped the drugs off with Kingston then drove off heading to the Penthouse to talk with Justine.

As Dirty pulled in the parking lot, he saw Monica's car parked in the parking lot. Dirty called the house phone, blocking his number so they wouldn't see that it was him calling. The phone rang.

"Hello?"

"Who is this," Dirty asked disguising his voice.

"Who do you want to talk to?"

"Justine!"

"This is her; who is this?"

Click – as Dirty hung up!

Dirty didn't understand why Justine was still there.

Dirty had given his word to Speedy, but wasn't for sure if Speedy could maintain after all that had happened. Dirty had to be careful because now he realized that he wasn't the only Dirty Cop that worked the streets of Charlotte.

Dirty's main concern was that they knew what they claimed and that there was a possibility that he might be facing murder charges.

Dirty still had some unfinished work to take care of.

ABOUT THE AUTHOR

Devon Sturdivant was raised on the streets as a young delinquent who thought the streets were the solution to everything that life had to offer.

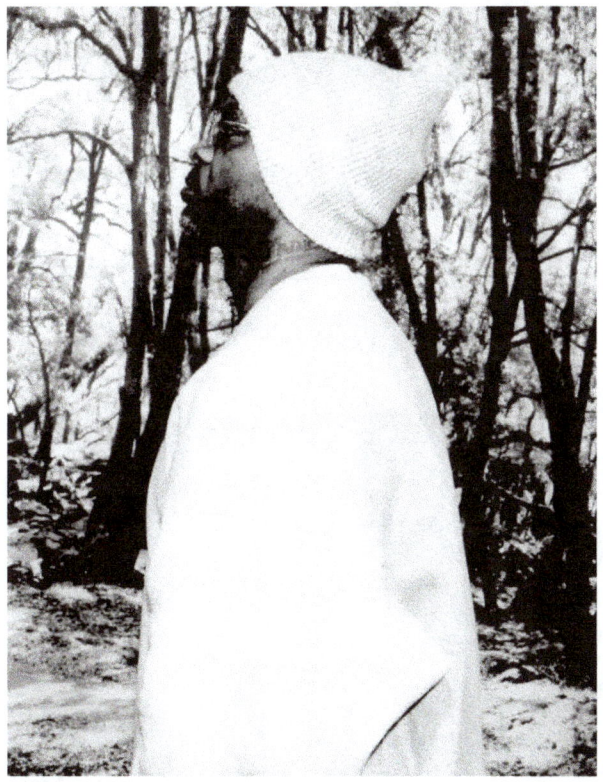

Being incarcerated part of his life, he can honestly say that he wouldn't wish it on a dog that has to be locked up or caged.

He's learned through his struggle that it's more important that you know exactly what you want and expect out of life. Have a closer evaluation of self, and know your goals. Whether your goals are short or long-term, follow your dreams, and believe in your heart because you will never know if you don't try.

Devon misses being a father to his children and doing all the things a father is supposed to do to provide for them. They are his motivation and inspiration to establish the very best for them.

Devon has eight other books that are coming behind this one. Be on the lookout for Dirty Cop II coming later this year.

If anyone has any comments or would like to write the author about the book, we encourage you to do so.

Devon Sturdivant #20847-058
Federal Medical Center
POBox 14500
Lexington, KY   40512

Coming soon!

More of the Hottest Fiction Books from the Best of Friend

Dirty Cop 2

Dirty Cop 3

Lunatic Rises 1

Lunatic Rises 2

One Last Lick

Life's a Gamble

You may order more copies of this book and/or copies of Leonard McCoy's first book, Born To Be A Gangster, using this order form or logging onto:

MidnightExpressBooks.com

QTY	Title	Price Each	
_____	Secrets of a Dirty Cop I	$14.95	_____
_____	Born To Be A Gangster	$14.95	_____

Shipping
___ books ordered @ $3.99/Each   _____

TOTAL ENCLOSED   _____

Please send check or money order to:

Midnight Express Books
POBox 69
Berryville, AR 72616

NAME: _____

ADDRESS: _____

CITY: _____ STATE _____ ZIP _____

www.ingramcontent.com/pod-product-compliance
Lightning Source LLC
Chambersburg PA
CBHW071253170626
46809CB00001B/198